How can a brilliant detective shine in the dark?

How can a brilliant detective shine in the dark?

LINDA BAILEY

KIDS CAN PRESS

Kids Can Press acknowledges the financial support of the Ontario Arts Council, the Canada Council for the Arts and the Government of Canada, through the BPIDP, for our publishing activity.

Published in Canada by
Kids Can Press Ltd.
29 Birch Avenue
Toronto, ON M4V 1E2

Published in the U.S. by
Kids Can Press Ltd.
2250 Military Road
Tonawanda, NY 14150

www.kidscanpress.com

Edited by Charis Wahl
Typeset by Karen Birkemoe
Printed and bound in Canada

CM 03 0 9 8 7 6 5 4 3 2 1
CM PA 99 0 9 8 7 6 5 4 3

National Library of Canada Cataloguing in Publication Data

Bailey, Linda, 1948–
  How can a brilliant detective shine in the dark

(A Stevie Diamond mystery ; 6)
ISBN 1-55074-896-3 (bound).   ISBN 1-55074-750-9 (pbk.)

I. Title. II. Series: Bailey, Linda, 1948–   .
Stevie Diamond mystery ; 6.

PS8553.A3644H58 1999   jC813'.54   C99-931361-4
PZ7.B1526Ho 1999

Kids Can Press is a *lOrUs*™ Entertainment company

This book is for Anna and Jesse Koeller,
long-time friends and as close as family.

Thanks to my daughter, Tess Grainger, for her
thoughtful reading and astute comments on the
draft manuscript. Thanks to Charis Wahl for
another fine edit and for hanging out with
Stevie, Jesse and me through all these years.

CHAPTER

E VEN AN EXPERIENCED DETECTIVE CAN MISS
things.
Take me, for example. Stevie Diamond,
girl detective, just turned thirteen. In the past
year, I've brought five crooks to justice. I've been
thanked by the police, congratulated by the
mayor and interviewed on the six o'clock news.
All that, and I *still* didn't see the freight-train-sized
mystery that was sitting there, right in the middle
of my own family!

At least … I didn't see it at first.

It all began with Uncle Archie.

He was the uncle who ran off to Europe to join
the circus, way back before I was born. Nobody
ever talked about him much, and anyway, he was
my mother's uncle, not mine. Who pays attention
to their mother's uncle?

So I never gave Uncle Archie a thought – not
until my mom and I were on the ferry boat heading
for Catriola Island. Catriola is where Aunt Edna and
Aunt Ivy live. They're my mom's aunts, and they'd
organized a family reunion to welcome Uncle

Archie home. For most of the family, it would be a first introduction. Uncle Archie had been gone for forty-five years.

Wait a minute!

Did I say forty-five years? Without a single visit? That *alone* should have made me suspicious.

But even on the ferry, it took me ages to clue in. First, I checked the lifeboats, just to make sure this wasn't a *Titanic*-type situation. Then my mom and I had a snack in the cafeteria – fries and gravy for me, clam chowder for her. Back on deck, we watched a seagull flying into the wind. Seagulls aren't the brightest birds, I've noticed. This one was just about flapping its feathers off, trying to keep up with the boat.

It wasn't until we'd done all those things that I noticed my mom seemed … well, lost in her own thoughts.

"Mom? Hey, Mom. MOM!"

"Hmmm … yes, Stevie?" She was staring out at the ocean. Greenish saltwater with ribbons of foam on top. Murky. Dark. Deep.

"Mind if I swim back to Vancouver? I passed Level 6 in swim class."

"Mmmm … if you like."

"For Pete's sake, Mom! Hel-LO!"

She blinked, shook her head and looked at me – really looked – for the first time since we'd gotten on the boat. Her wiry brown hair whipped around her face. I waited while she pulled a strand out of her mouth.

"I guess … I was thinking about Uncle Archie," she said.

"What about him?"

"Oh … well … nothing." Her eyes glazed over again.

The first wrinkle of suspicion stirred in my brain.

It was the word "nothing." That was exactly what everybody always said about Uncle Archie. Nothing! Nobody ever really *talked* about the guy. Not even Aunt Ivy and Aunt Edna, and they were his sisters. What made it even stranger was that the aunts loved to gossip, especially about relatives. It was almost a hobby. So how come Uncle Archie's name never came up?

I thought back to the couple of times I'd asked about him. The answers were five words long, max. Once, I dug a picture of him out of an old box of photos – a little kid sitting on a fence. Aunt Ivy's eyes got all teary when she saw it. Aunt Edna clenched her teeth so tight that her chin stuck out like a bulldog's. But they didn't *say* a word.

Something was definitely going on here.

When in doubt, ask.

"So what's the story, Mom? On Uncle Archie."

For a moment, I thought I was going to get another "nothing." Instead, she gave me a searching look and nodded.

"Something happened," she said quietly. "All those years ago. Before Uncle Archie left."

Bingo! I held my breath. "What?"

She shrugged and rubbed her upper arms, which were covered in goose bumps in spite of the summer sun. "That's what's bothering me. I don't know."

I waited. Sometimes if you're trying to get information and you say too much, the person you're talking to clams up. Silent Stevie, that was me.

It worked.

"All I know is – back when I was a girl, when I spent my summers on the island – Aunt Ivy used to have nightmares." My mom was staring at the water again, looking sort of hypnotized. Excellent. People in a trance talk freely.

"She had the same nightmare over and over. She would call out in her sleep, 'Archie! Archie!' Sometimes I went into her room to wake her up. She'd be mumbling and moaning all kinds of things – I couldn't tell what – but she seemed to be trying to help Archie. To save him."

"From what?"

She shook her head. "I don't know."

To me, the next step was obvious. "So let's ask her!"

That got my mom's attention. Her head whipped around, and she held up a warning finger. "Don't you dare, Stevie!"

I shrugged. "Why not? You always say that the only way to find out about things is to ask."

"I say that about math! About science! This is different. If Aunt Ivy and Aunt Edna don't want to talk about why Archie left, then we are *not* going to drive them crazy with questions. Got it?"

I nodded. *We* – me and my mom – were definitely not going to drive them crazy with questions. *I*, on the other hand …

"Good." My mom pointed off the front of the

ferry. A wooden dock was coming into view. "We're almost there, so let's get a few ground rules straight. One – no complaining about the food."

I felt my face twist into a grimace. Somehow I had managed to get all this way without thinking about Aunt Edna's cooking – a serious mistake. I should have eaten a full-meal special in the cafeteria. I should have ordered a bunch of desserts to go. My mood took a sudden dive.

"Two – be nice to your cousins."

The cousins. The thought of *them* made my mood drop even lower. I think it ended up in my shoes.

My mom must have heard my teeth grinding. "It's only for a few days, Stevie."

I grunted. A few days with the cousins could feel like a *decade*.

"How come Dad didn't have to come?"

"I told you. He couldn't get away from work. Besides, somebody has to look after Radical."

Radical's our cat. I pictured the two of them, my dad and Radical, lying around on the couch, eating takeout pizza and watching baseball on TV. They were probably cheering a home run right this minute.

Not fair.

"Oh, look!" My mom's face lit up as she pointed. "There they are! Aunt Edna and Aunt Ivy and – and that must be Uncle Archie."

Uncle Archie? I perked up.

Peering at the spot on the dock where my mom pointed, I could see the aunts – Aunt Ivy thin and birdlike, Aunt Edna squat, like a human fire hydrant. They were both waving, and Aunt Ivy was doing these funny little excited jumps. In between them was someone I'd never seen before. A man. He wasn't waving – just rocking back and forth, back and forth, heels to toes, heels to toes.

There he was – the mysterious Uncle Archie.

Y MOM AND I HURRIED TO JOIN THE OTHER passengers who were waiting to walk off the ferry. Out of nowhere, my mom started humming. Some people twitch when they get nervous. My mom hums.

She was still humming as the ramp went down and as we walked across it to land. When Aunt Ivy saw us coming, she started waving and jumping up and down again. She was wearing a floppy skirt and a baggy red T-shirt, and she held a canvas hat over her frizzy gray hair.

"Yoo-hoo! Here we are. Valerie, Stevie. Over here!"

There were only three other people on the dock, so she didn't really *need* to yell. But Aunt Ivy's the enthusiastic type.

I looked at Aunt Edna, waiting for her to tell Aunt Ivy to for-heaven's-sake-pipe-down. But Aunt Edna seemed excited too. Her square face was flushed a bright pink, and she kept clutching at her carefully ironed gray skirt, scrunching it in her hands.

Between them stood Uncle Archie. I don't know what I was expecting. Somebody wild-and-crazy-looking, I guess — a cross between Renaldo the sword swallower and Bozo the clown.

Instead, there was this totally grandpa-looking guy — the kind you'd see at a school science fair standing beside his grandson's display saying, "I used to be a science whiz myself. I bet that's where Sonny here gets his talent." His eyes had soft pouches underneath and crinkles at the sides, and his bald head gleamed in the sun. He wore a pale blue golf shirt with a kangaroo on the pocket and a pair of those loose grandpa-type pants with the stretchy waist. The only thing missing for the total grandpa look was a potbelly. Uncle Archie was thin, with ropy-looking arms.

Aunt Ivy and Aunt Edna started introducing him at the same time. It came out all in a jumble. After a minute, Uncle Archie took one of my mom's hands in both of his.

"Little Valerie?"

My mom stopped humming. "Welcome home, Uncle Archie." She gave him a peck on the cheek.

He smiled a big grandpa smile. "I haven't seen you since you were … well, about that high." He held up a hand at knee level. "You were always dragging around a one-eyed teddy bear. You remember that bear?"

"Pim!" exclaimed Aunt Edna. "*You* remember, Valerie. He got so shabby and dirty that we tried to make you hand him over for a cleaning and a new eye. But you wouldn't."

Aunty Ivy clasped her thin hands together in

front of her chest. "You *loved* that bear, Valerie."

My mother's forehead wrinkled. I could see she didn't have a clue who Pim the one-eyed teddy bear was. She smiled anyway. "What a wonderful memory you have, Uncle Archie."

"Well, you're a hard little girl to forget. But this girl now!" He turned to me. "I sure don't have any memories of her. Could this be Stephanie?"

"Stevie," I said. "Nobody calls me Stephanie anymore."

Aunt Edna made a little harrumphing noise.

"Except for Aunt Edna," I added quickly. "*She* calls me Stephanie."

Aunt Edna started muttering under her breath. "What kind of a name is Stevie? Some kind of boy's name? Some kind of a truck driver?"

There were hugs all around. Then Aunt Ivy threw an arm around my shoulders and started moving me toward the car. "We're so glad you could come, Stevie. Natalie and the twins are already here. And little Hugo, of course."

The cousins. Oy!

I gave her my best imitation of a smile.

The aunts' car was one of those huge ones they built a long time ago, with big fins on the back and tons of chrome on the sides. My dad called it a "boat." But as Aunt Edna said, what did they need with a new car when they hardly ever left the island?

Personally, I liked it. The seats were wide enough to hold four people, and they were covered in red plush upholstery that you could sink right into. I climbed in the back with my mom and Aunt Edna. Uncle Archie sat in the front passenger seat, and Aunt Ivy got behind the wheel.

Aunty Ivy doesn't like driving. It makes her nervous. The only reason she does it is because somebody has to. Aunt Edna *can't* drive because she refuses to wear her glasses. She says they spoil her looks. If you could see Aunt Edna, you'd know how funny that is.

Anyway, you'd think being nervous would make Aunt Ivy slow and careful. Think again. It makes her want to get the ride over with as quickly as possible.

Grabbing the wheel in a grip of iron, Aunt Ivy leaned forward, hunched her shoulders and gunned it. Loose gravel sprayed the road behind us. We tore across the island so fast that the scenery – tall trees, rocky beaches, community hall, Priddy's General Store – was nothing but a blur. Fortunately, there aren't many cars on Catriola Island, and they all know enough to pull over when they see Aunt Ivy coming.

Aunt Edna tried to get her to slow down, yelling instructions from the back. But once Aunt Ivy's moving, it's like she's deaf.

Eventually we screeched into a long driveway with a sign out front that said "The Coopers." Aunt Ivy finally slowed down as we wound our way through a narrow, twisting tunnel of firs and cedars. The driveway opened onto a large meadow with an orchard on one side, a garden on the other, and a small wooden house front and center. The house was covered in cedar shingles that had gone gray. It had a big old-fashioned porch.

The relatives were waiting on the porch as we pulled up. Aunt Patricia, Aunt Cheryl and ...

Argh! The cousins. Natalie. The twins. Little Hugo.

Maybe they'd changed?

Hugo ran across the lawn on stubby bare legs, his toddler diaper drooping. *He'd* changed. The last time I saw him, he could hardly crawl, never mind run. He spoiled his new act by belly-flopping on the grass, but when he got up, he was still grinning. Like most of the people in my mom's family, Hugo has thick curly hair. My dad calls it "Cooper hair." Hugo's rises from his head in a reddish cloud. I grinned back at him and gave him a little tap on the nose. Hugo was okay.

Kenneth and Kevin – the twins, nine years old – followed more slowly. They were dressed, as usual, in identical outfits. Today they were wearing green-and-yellow checked shirts, brown shorts, sandals and, of course, socks. The twins *always* wear socks. They probably even wear them in the shower.

"Hi, Kenneth," I said. "Hi, Kevin."

I was careful to stare right between them as I spoke. Besides wearing identical clothes, the twins also wear their hair exactly the same. Really short and parted on the left. It's impossible to tell them apart.

"Hi, Stevie," they said together.

"Want to play Go Fish?" asked the one on the right.

Nope. They hadn't changed. Their only interest was playing cards. Not just any cards either. They *only* liked Go Fish. I was hoping they might have branched out.

"Sure, Kevin," I said, trying to be a good sport. "Maybe later."

"I'm Kenneth," he said.

"Yeah, right. Kenneth."

The last cousin, Natalie, was talking to my mom. Natalie also had Cooper hair. It fell in long waves past her shoulders. "Aunty Valerie, the most fabulous thing has happened. This new mall just opened up right behind our house. It has all the *best* stores. Denim City and Caroline's Cupboard and –"

"Hi, Natalie," I said.

"– Sporty Girl and Shoes to Die For and ..."

Natalie's only two years older than me. She used to be okay. But some time in the last couple of years, she'd decided that she was grown up – and I wasn't. I guess that hadn't changed either.

My mom's sisters – Aunt Cheryl and Aunt Patricia – each gave me a hug. Aunt Cheryl, the mom of Hugo and the twins, had to reach up to hug me. She said the thing *all* adults say these days if they haven't seen me for a while.

"Stevie! You're so tall!"

It's hard to know what to answer. Oh really, I hadn't noticed?

"Yes, I am tall," I agreed. "I certainly have grown." I looked around. "Where's Uncle Bob?"

"He couldn't get away from work," she said. "Besides, someone had to look after Tiger."

Tiger. Their cat. Sure.

"Are you ready to play Go Fish now?" The voice came from right beside me. One of the twins was standing really close, staring up into my left ear. Kenneth? Kevin?

"In a minute," I said. "Right now, I want to ..."

What? What could I do to get out of playing Go Fish?

I remembered. Uncle Archie! He'd been in the circus, right?

"Hey, Uncle Archie! Did you learn any tricks in the circus? Like ... I don't know ... walking the high wire or swinging on the trapeze? Stuff like that?"

Uncle Archie grinned, his eyes crinkling. "Well, after all these years, I guess I must have learned something."

Great!

"Could you show us, Uncle Archie?"

This got the rest of them going. Kevin and Kenneth started saying, "Yeah, yeah, show us," and Natalie forgot how grownup she was supposed to be and latched on to his arm, begging, "Oh please, Uncle Archie. That would be wicked." Even Hugo, who could hardly talk, got caught up in the excitement and started hopping around, yelling, "So! So!" which I figured was his version of "show."

Uncle Archie shrugged and let himself be led to the open area in front of the porch. Rubbing his chin, he looked around thoughtfully. Meanwhile, everybody – adults included – found a chair or railing or step to sit on.

"Hmmm," said Uncle Archie. "Do we happen to have a few oranges around?"

Aunt Ivy jumped up and ran into the house, returning with a net bag full of oranges. The next thing you knew, Uncle Archie had three of them whirling in circles in front of him. Then he grabbed a fourth and juggled it too. Then a fifth. Then he switched directions. Then he juggled them behind his back. And under one leg.

Hugo screeched with excitement. The rest of us clapped and hooted.

Uncle Archie stopped juggling and bowed. He turned to Aunt Ivy. "I don't suppose you happen to have a few flaming torches handy?"

Aunt Ivy's mouth dropped open.

Uncle Archie laughed. "Just kidding. Although I *can* juggle flaming torches. Knives too."

He gave me a wink, then glanced toward a tall wooden fence. It looked old but sturdy.

Before you could say Ringling Brothers Circus, Uncle Archie was on the top rail. But not the way you or I would be up there. Oh no. Uncle Archie made that railing look like a dance floor. He pranced back and forth like a ballet dancer. He jumped. He twirled. His small, narrow feet never took a step out of place.

I looked down at my own feet. Size 9. Then I glanced over at my mom's. Lucky for Archie, he hadn't inherited the Cooper family clodhoppers. Although maybe, on a *real* tightrope, big feet would be an advantage. More foot to grip the wire with, right?

Moments later, he hopped gracefully down

from the fence. My mom and I exchanged glances, and I knew we were thinking the same thing. Uncle Archie sure didn't act his age.

After doing a little bow, he asked Aunt Ivy if there was a bicycle around. When she brought out an old three-speed, he jumped on and started riding it in circles around the yard.

Doesn't sound like much, I know, except – he was sitting on it backward.

That's right. Backward!

Then he turned around forward and asked if any of the kids wanted to "come aboard." Well, naturally, we all did. And one by one, as he rode in circles, Uncle Archie loaded us kids onto that bike. All except Hugo, who was too little. By the end, one twin was hanging off each side, Natalie was hanging off the back, and I was sitting on the handlebars. Uncle Archie told me to stick my leg up and point my toe. It was like a real circus act – the Flying Cooper Family!

The grown-ups were all yelling and cheering. Hugo was hollering too. "Me want! Me want! Me want!"

Uncle Archie told the rest of us to jump down, and he gave Hugo his own little ride, holding him in one arm while he steered the bike with the other. Hugo stuck his leg out in the air the way he'd seen me do it. Of all the tricks so far, we cheered loudest for that one.

"Uncle Archie, that was wonderful!" said my mom, still clapping as he climbed off the bike.

"Glad you enjoyed it." Uncle Archie waved away my mom's compliments, but he was sweating and puffing a little, so I guess it wasn't as easy as it looked. The aunts must have noticed too, because they insisted that he come inside and rest.

The cousins and I followed the adults in, and we all sat around the living room, eating rock-hard Edna-cookies and drinking tea. Everyone started asking Uncle Archie questions about his life in the circus. It took me a few minutes to realize what this was – a golden opportunity to work in a few questions of my own about the mysterious "something" that had "happened" all those years ago.

"Hey, Uncle Archie," I said. "What made you decide to join the circus? Was it a sudden decision, or what?"

Until that moment, I didn't know there was such a thing as a loud silence. This one was deafening. I didn't look at my mom, but I could feel her glare burning into my cheek like a hot iron.

Uncle Archie stretched his arms slowly above his head. "Gosh, Stevie, it was such a long time ago. I suppose I just wanted an adventure."

He might have said more, but Aunty Ivy jumped in. "Speaking of adventure, did Edna and I tell you about our bus trip to Seattle? We went with the Catriola Seniors Group, and if you want to hear about *adventure* ..."

And that was that. Before long, the grown-ups were talking about Great-Great-Grandpa, who had died in the war, and Great-Great-Grandma, who had been the best quilter on Catriola Island. Then they got onto the eastern branch of the Cooper family, who were still living in Pickering, running a dairy farm and … well, it was time for any kid with half a brain to leave.

I wandered out into the yard with a twin right behind me. The bicycle was still lying on the ground.

"Hey, Kenneth," I said, "want to try riding double on the bike?"

"It's Kevin." He shook his head no.

"Aw, come on. Just once. I'll ride, and you can sit on the handlebars."

"Uh-uh."

The other twin wandered out, cookie in hand. Natalie followed. Flopping down on a wicker chair, she pulled a bottle of nail polish out of her bag and started painting her nails. I invited her and Kenneth to try the bike with me.

"Uh-uh," said Kenneth.

Natalie gave me the kind of look you'd give someone who'd just suggested a trip to Pluto.

"Fine," I muttered. "I'll do it myself."

I rode the old bike around the yard twice, taking careful note of all the bumps, holes and buried rocks in the ground. Then, figuring I'd had enough practice, I got off and climbed on again.

Backward.

Whooooooooooaaaaaaaa!

For the first three seconds, it was great – more exciting than a roller coaster and at least as scary.

Then it was over.

"Did it hurt, Stevie?" The twins stood above me, side by side, staring down. From where I sat – lay, actually – they looked like a matched set of salt and pepper shakers.

"Hardly at all," I lied. Slowly, I untangled my legs from the metal. I rubbed the spot on my backside where a softball-sized bruise was getting started.

"Anybody want to try fence-walking?" I asked.

The twins shook their heads. How *did* they *do* that – move their heads in exactly the same direction at exactly the same time? Did they practice?

Brushing grass and dirt off my clothes, I headed for the fence. I had walked plenty of fences. It couldn't be that hard. True, I had never tried *this* fence before. It was shoulder-high and – as I discovered when I gave it a push – a wee bit shaky. Lucky for me, I have terrific balance.

"Upsy-daisy!"

Upsy-daisy went really well. Unfortunately, I was only halfway through upsy-daisy when downsy-doozy started. I clutched frantically at the fence, then the air –

"Did *that* hurt, Stevie?"

"NO!"

"You don't have to yell," said Kevin. Or maybe Kenneth.

"You're going to break something," Natalie added without looking up. "Your neck, probably."

Well, okay. Maybe I *should* try something safer. I headed for the oranges.

Juggling turned out to be safe, all right, but no easier than Uncle Archie's other tricks. After ten minutes of practice, the ground was littered with cracked-open oranges. The twins gazed at them in silence.

"Aunt Edna's not going to like that," said Natalie from the porch.

"Want to play Go Fish?" asked a twin. He and his brother stared at me blankly, their pudgy arms hanging limp at their sides.

Oh, what was the point? Bending over, I started picking up oranges. "Sure, Kevin. Why not? Let's play Go Fish."

"Kenneth," he said.

"Whatever."

For the rest of the day, I played Go Fish with the twins. Two out of the three of us were very, very happy.

Dinner was a typical Aunty Edna meal. I won't torture you with the details, but if I tell you that the best part was the mashed turnips, you'll get the idea. The brown gooey stuff was meatloaf — that's what my mom said when I asked her later. The white soupy stuff was potatoes. Aunt Edna must have cooked them for hours to get them to dissolve like that.

At least there were no weird surprises. One of the problems with Aunt Edna doing the cooking — and not wearing her glasses — is that sometimes she makes mistakes. The vanilla bottle and the soya sauce bottle, for instance, sort of look alike.

Soya sauce cupcakes. Vanilla chow mein. Think about it.

I did my best *not* to think about it. Shoveling in as much Edna-food as I could stand, I concentrated on the conversation at the table.

The aunts had invited a neighbor for dinner — Hank Dooley. He and Uncle Archie had been best friends when they were kids. Uncle Archie started rattling off the things they used to do together – build treehouses, swing on branches in the woods, fish, swim, make fires. He told lots of stories, and they *should* have been interesting. But somehow they weren't. Not much expression, if you know what I mean. He sounded like someone giving a report at school.

I waited for Hank to tell us what *he* remembered, but he just chewed on his lip and listened. A strange old guy, Hank, all sharp angles – knees, elbows, nose, chin. He had long curly yellow-gray hair that grew every which way and a huge yellow-white mustache that seemed to be trying to crawl into his mouth.

Living all alone in a little cabin on the beach must have made Hank shy because he never spoke up much in company. I tried to imagine him as a little boy, yelling and swinging on branches, but it was hard. It was even harder to imagine him and Uncle Archie as best friends. They seemed so different.

Thinking about best friends made me think about *my* best friend. Jesse Kulniki. He and I are pretty different too. (For one thing, Jesse wouldn't be eating this meatloaf I was pushing around my plate. Not now. Not ever. Jesse's a vegetarian.) He lives a few doors away from me, so he's my neighbor as well as my friend. For the past year or so, he's been my detecting partner too.

I pictured Jesse, back home in Vancouver, packing to go to Caribou Ranch Resort. He and his mom would be leaving the next day. The brochure he'd shown me said the resort had horses, swimming pools, hot tubs and hiking trails. Gourmet food too.

Looking down at my meatloaf, I sighed. Now I knew why I'd been such a grouch with Jesse before I left. Jealousy, plain and simple. When he'd mentioned horseback riding, I'd brought up horsefly bites. When he'd talked about the gourmet food, I'd mentioned fish eggs and chicken livers.

Suddenly I felt really crummy. Jesse never treated *me* that way. When my baseball team made the finals and his didn't, Jesse was happy for me. He even came to my games and cheered. But me? Well, what could I say? I was a Lousy Friend. Nothing I could do about it now either. Unless ...

"Mom? Can I phone Jesse?"

She thought for a moment. "It's long distance, sweetie." Then she thought again. "Well, okay, if you charge the call to our home number and don't stay on too long."

"I promise."

Seconds later, I was talking to Jesse. He sounded so *normal* after the cousins.

"Hey, Stevie! What's up? How's the holiday?"

"It's ... fine," I said. "But that's not what I wanted to talk about. Listen, I'm sorry I said all those things about Caribou Ranch Resort. I'm sure you and your mom will –"

"We're not going."

"What?"

"We're not going." He sounded really unhappy.

"They phoned from the resort. There are forest fires burning all around it. They might even have to evacuate. They've canceled all the new people coming in – like us."

"Oh." I couldn't think of what to say.

"It stinks, Stevie."

I nodded. Then, realizing he couldn't see me, I said, "You're right. It does."

"My mom says she'll take time off later in the summer and we'll try somewhere else. But for now, she's going back to work. And me? I'm just sitting around here, staring at my toenails."

Better than at the twins' socks, I thought. Then – wait a minute!

"JESSE!"

"Ow, Stevie. That hurt my ear."

"Listen to me. You can come here! To Catriola Island!"

"What?"

"I mean it. You can take the ferry over, and we'll meet you, and you can stay here and – it'll be great."

There was a pause. "What's it like there?"

"Oh … well, Uncle Archie's really something. Remember I told you he was in the circus? He does all these great circus tricks. Juggling. Tight-rope walking. And the island has beaches and forests and –"

What else did he like? Birds! Jesse was interested in birds.

"Plenty of interesting birds!" I finished, remembering the seagull above the ferry. I had also spotted a sparrow in front of the house. "It's practically Bird Island."

"Sounds great. But, uh, don't you have to ask?"

"Hold on."

My mom was busy being family photographer. She had the twins and Hugo posed together on the couch. Her forehead furrowed when I asked about Jesse. She said we were guests ourselves, and another person would make more work for the aunts. But Aunt Ivy overheard and said, "Nonsense, Valerie! We'll hardly even notice him in this crowd. Stevie, you go right ahead and invite your friend. Tell him we'll put some country roses in his cheeks."

I went back to the phone. "Aunty Ivy's going to put roses in your cheeks."

"What?"

"Never mind. You can come. My mom wants to talk to your mom."

A few minutes later, it was all arranged. Jesse's mom would put him on the ferry the next day. We'd meet him in the afternoon the same way the aunts had met us.

I was feeling pretty cheerful as I helped my mom drag the aunts' old tent out of the garage. With the house being so small and Uncle Archie visiting, there wasn't much room for people to sleep inside. Natalie was sharing Aunt Ivy's room, but the rest of us were going to camp out.

This suited me just fine. I asked my mom if we could set up our tent at the far end of the meadow, near a clump of tall birch trees. There was a stream back there too.

"Good idea," said my mom. "We won't hear Hugo if he wakes up in the middle of the night."

As we put up the tent, the birch leaves shivered in the wind and the meadow grasses quivered. I felt so happy I could have giggled. This spot was perfect – far enough from the house that we would feel almost as if we were on a camping trip. Jesse was a city kind of guy – nervous about bears and so on – but we'd camped together before, and I knew he liked the *idea* of the wilderness. This corner of the meadow would be just right.

Later, lying in my sleeping bag beside my mom, I listened to the wind, the burbles of the stream, and the rustles, creaks and croaks that make up nighttime on the island. A cool breeze wafted through the window screen and danced across my face and hair, making me shiver even though the rest of my body was feather-bed warm.

I love tents.

My mind drifted back through the day. I thought about Uncle Archie's circus tricks and how they were a *lot* harder than they looked. Then I thought about Uncle Archie's mysterious past – the "something" that had "happened" before he left. I still hadn't found out much about that. In fact, I hadn't found out anything.

Never mind. Jesse was on his way. Between the two of us, we had tons of detecting experience. A little case like this, with no complications? We'd wrap it up in no time. Piece of cake.

Cake? Argh! That's the *last* thing you should think about after one of Aunty Edna's meals.

Too late now. There it was in my mind. Thick.

Gooey. Three layers of dark chocolate. Vanilla icing. Chocolate sprinkles and pink roses on top.

I don't *really* believe in mental telepathy. I don't *really* think you can send someone messages in your thoughts. But it was worth a try.

I concentrated hard. Jesse would probably be in bed now. *Bring cake*, I signaled, sending the message on what I hoped was a fairly direct brain-to-brain route. *Bring chocolate cake to Catriola Island.*

"Whussat?" My mom's voice was drowsy. "You say something, Stevie?"

"No, Mom. Nothing. Go to sleep."

"'Night," she said.

Holding a hand over my mouth to make sure no sounds came out, I finished the message.

Sprinkles. Roses. Big!

CHAPTER

I WAS HOPING TO CATCH UNCLE ARCHIE ALONE IN THE morning. If I could ambush him on the porch or something, maybe we could have a little heart-to-heart talk about his mysterious past. But he'd gone out early. "For a walk," said Aunt Ivy.

So I had to find another way to pass the time until Jesse showed up on the afternoon ferry. A book would have been good. Back in Vancouver, thinking ahead about the aunts' house, I had packed a bag of the most exciting-sounding books I could find. *The Mummy Walks at Midnight. Murder at Soccer Camp. Frankenstein's Last Call*. It was a great collection.

And it was still sitting on my bed at home.

Rats!

There was a stack of magazines on the coffee table. I checked them out, but they all had names like *Country Crafts* or *Gardening Life*. A whole wall of the living room was covered with shelves, but the books were old and about tomato growing or faraway countries or lives-of-famous-people-you-never-heard-of.

The aunts didn't have a TV or a computer either. What was left was … Go Fish.

"Listen, guys, I know this *other* game. It's called Hearts. You'd like it."

Kenneth, or maybe Kevin, smiled. "We like Go Fish."

The twins were neon bright today, in matching orange striped T-shirts with yellow shorts. Socks, of course. Green ones. And running shoes so white they almost glowed.

"Yeah, but don't you think it's fun to try something new?"

Kevin, or maybe Kenneth, shook his head. "Nope."

When Uncle Archie finally turned up, just after lunch, we were on our twenty-eighth game of Go Fish.

"Hey there, Uncle Archie!" I said. "Where did you go?"

He swelled up his chest and patted it. "Getting a breath of fresh air."

Fresh air? On Catriola? The island is nothing *but* fresh air. Why would he have to go off alone to get some? But before I could ask, he disappeared to his room for a nap.

The afternoon – more Go Fish – seemed to last forever. Finally it was time for Aunt Ivy and me to get in the old car and pick up Jesse. Aunt Ivy hunkered over the wheel, turned a few shades paler – you could actually *see* her skin change – and then hit the gas pedal, hard. We shot across the island in silence. I figured it was safer that way.

When Jesse stepped off the ferry, I almost giggled with happiness. Twenty-four hours with the cousins had made him look like the winning ticket in a lottery. He was carrying a backpack and wearing a wrinkled white T-shirt, sloppy cutoffs and faded running shoes. No socks. He hadn't combed his hair either. It stuck up in eight different directions.

"Yoo-hoo, Jesse! Over here!"

Oh my gosh. I sounded just like Aunty Ivy!

Jesse and I slapped hands. Aunt Ivy welcomed him with a curtsey-like bob and a smile. Then I helped him get his backpack off, checking for cake-shaped boxes inside.

"Did you bring me anything?" I whispered.

Jesse looked confused. Then a light went on. "Oh yeah!" he said. "Yeah, I did."

I wiggled my eyebrows at him. He grinned and wiggled back.

Unbelievable! Mental telepathy actually worked!

I meant to warn Jesse about Aunty Ivy's driving, I really did, but I didn't get a chance. As we roared across the island, his mouth kept opening and closing like a goldfish. Every time we peeled around a sharp curve, he clung, two-handed, to the armrest. I don't think he noticed the scenery at all.

When we finally reached the house, he tottered shakily out of the car. "What's she doing?" he whispered. "Practicing for the Indy 500?"

"No," I whispered back. "She's scared of driving."

"She's – what? Are you kidding me?"

"Shhh! She'll hear you."

"*She's* scared? *She's* scared?"

There was a sudden roar behind us, and the car did a couple of lurches – in our direction. Jesse screeched and leaped out of the way.

"Sorry, kids!" Aunt Ivy called cheerily from behind the wheel. "I thought it was turned off."

I hurried Jesse through the introductions to the relatives. Still in shock, he didn't take much notice until we got to the cousins. I guess I'd forgotten to mention that Kenneth and Kevin were twins. Jesse blinked a couple of times as if he was seeing double. Then he nodded at them. Twice.

"Hi. Hi."

"Want to play Go Fish?"

Jesse perked up. "I *love* Go Fish."

Uh-oh. Something else I hadn't warned Jesse about.

"Later," I told the twins. "Jesse has to unpack first."

The only relative Jesse didn't meet was Uncle Archie. He was out walking again. Sucking up more of that fresh island air? This Uncle Archie was turning out to be a real outdoorsy guy.

Aunt Ivy searched the garage and came up with a small orange tent for Jesse. He carried it across the meadow to our camping spot while I lugged his backpack, smiling at the thought of its secret cargo. I still couldn't believe the mental telepathy had worked.

"So?" I said, propping the backpack carefully against a large rock. "Where is it?"

"Where's what?"

"The cake."

"What cake?"

"The cake I asked you to bring. Chocolate? Vanilla icing? With sprinkles?"

He made a face. "What are you talking about?"

Rats!

"Jesse Kulniki, do you mean to tell me there's no cake in this backpack?"

He held out his hands, palms up. "Do I look like a bakery? *What* are you talking about?"

"You said you brought me something."

"Oh, that. Just a second." He began hauling things out of his backpack. Swimsuit. Pajamas. Peanuts. Towel. Pillowcase. Colored pencils. Apple. T-shirt. Bathrobe. Small scruffy stuffed pig in sailor hat, which he shoved back inside really quickly. Shorts. Socks. Slippers. Calculator.

Calculator?

"Nothing wrong with being prepared," he said, spotting my expression. "Wait – here it is!"

He pulled out a crumpled, rolled-up piece of paper with an elastic band wrapped around it.

"Must have gotten a little squashed," he mumbled, unrolling it and trying to straighten out the crinkles.

I stared. It was a poster with big letters at the top. "Wild Birds of the West Coast." There were eagles on it. Woodpeckers. Hummingbirds. Herons. Ducks.

"You sounded so excited on the phone," said Jesse. "About birds! I was surprised, you know, because you never –"

"Very nice," I said, dropping the poster on the

ground and sticking my head inside the backpack. "You *sure* there's no cake?"

He looked puzzled. "What's the big deal about cake?"

I let out a sigh. "You'll see."

Back at the house, we were hardly in the door before the twins cornered Jesse, dragging him off for a game of Go Fish. Now that they had a new victim, they didn't even mind when I turned them down. And for the first hour or so, Jesse actually had fun. I sank into the old brown couch and leafed through *Good Housekeeping*, waiting for him to crack.

It took about an hour and a half.

"Hey, guys. Do you know how to play Rummy?" asked Jesse.

"Nope," said a twin.

"Oh. Well, how about Crazy Eights?"

"Nope."

"Old Maid?"

"Nope."

"Poker? Cribbage? War?"

"Nope."

Jesse looked back and forth between the twins, appealingly. "I could teach you those games. They're not hard."

"Nope."

Jesse threw a desperate glance my way. I shrugged.

"Hurry up, Jesse," said a twin. "It's your deal."

Just before dinner, Uncle Archie finally wandered in. He had mud on his boots and was puffing a little, so I figured he must have gone quite a ways to find that fresh air. When he came over to meet Jesse, he spotted the cards and offered to show us a few card tricks.

In one swift move, Jesse swept all the cards into a pile. Snatching the last few holdouts from Kenneth's hands, he said, "We'd love to, Mr. ... er ..."

"Call me Uncle Archie. I kind of like the sound of that."

It turned out that Uncle Archie's hands were as quick with cards as they were with oranges. Quicker! He could make cards appear and disappear from behind our ears. He could switch cards around on a table so fast it would make you dizzy. And he could *always* guess the card you picked from the middle of the deck without showing him.

"How do you do that?" asked Jesse.

"Trade secret," said Uncle Archie with a little wink.

The tricks ended when Aunt Ivy shooed us away from the table. She said she had to set it for dinner. Jesse's eyes brightened. They stayed bright right up until the food appeared.

"Hey, Stevie," he whispered. "What *is* this stuff?"

On the biggest plate was a large meaty lump, full of hunks of fat and gristle, sitting in a pool of greasy tomato liquid. I'd seen it before; Aunty Edna called it "brisket." Another bowl held peas ... I think. They'd lost their individual pea-ness, if you know what I mean, and were all mushed together. A third bowl held some shredded gray-ish stuff with brown flecks in it. There was also a green salad.

Aunt Edna was sitting directly across from Jesse.

Uh-oh.

"Hungry, Jesse?" she asked. Before he could answer, she loomed out of her chair, seized his plate, and dumped a large fatty hunk of brisket in the middle.

Jesse turned white.

"Um, Aunt Edna? Jesse's a vegetarian," I said.

She couldn't have looked more shocked if I'd said he was a centipede.

"Nonsense!" she trumpeted. "I've never heard such a foolish thing." She dumped a second lump of brisket on his plate for emphasis.

I looked around for my mom. She and Aunt Patricia were in the kitchen, pouring glasses of tomato juice.

Aunt Edna, meanwhile, was adding mushy peas and gray goop to Jesse's plate. He stared at the plate with a kind of horrified fascination, the way you might stare at a dead rat.

"Just look at the boy!" Aunty Edna said to Aunt Cheryl, who was sitting beside her, looking uncomfortable. "Skin and bones! Any fool can *see* he's starving. Well, not for long. We'll get some flesh on him before he goes back to the city."

Aunt Cheryl tried to change the subject. "This sauerkraut is wonderful, Aunt Edna. So ... tasty."

Sauerkraut? That must be the gray stuff with brown flecks.

Pointing at Jesse's plate, I whispered, "You can eat that. The sauerkraut. It's just cabbage."

He picked up a large forkful and stuffed it in his mouth, just as Aunt Edna said, "Of course it's tasty. I throw in half a pound of bacon!"

Oh.

Well, that explained the brown flecks.

On a scale of one to ten for politeness, Jesse would rank about a nine. The only thing anyone watching him would have noticed was his cheeks bulging out. Also his eyes, which did the same thing. Slowly, Jesse raised his napkin to his mouth. In one swift move, the cheeks caved in, the napkin swelled out, and the sauerkraut-filled napkin disappeared into his lap.

Beads of sweat dotted Jesse's forehead. He let out a couple of quick pants, like a dog.

Aunt Cheryl was still trying to keep Aunt Edna's mind off Jesse. She started talking about the island fair that was coming up, sounding fascinated as she asked about the pumpkin-growing competition.

"Try the salad," I whispered to Jesse.

Weakly, he reached for the greens and scooped some onto his plate. Picking up a forkful, he had it halfway to his mouth when he stopped. Stared.

I looked over. Perched on top of the lettuce, like a cowboy riding a horse, was a small white slug. As Jesse stared, it did a little wriggle to the left.

Okay, well, *this* was just bad luck. The lettuce was fresh from the garden. Aunt Edna must have washed it, but like I say, she wouldn't wear her glasses. This wasn't the first time a live bug had ended up in the salad. Too bad it had to happen now – to Jesse.

"Excuse me!" he blurted, lurching to his feet and charging toward the bathroom.

Aunt Edna squinted after him. Then she turned a fierce eye on me. "What's wrong with the boy?

Is he sick?"

I nodded. "Probably the flu."

It was a long time before Jesse came back. He looked calm enough, but I guess below the surface he was simmering, like a pot of water on low. By the time the meal ended, the water had heated up – to boiling.

"Why didn't you warn me?" he demanded the moment we were alone.

"Hey, come on," I said, trying a chuckle. "It's not *that* bad."

"Not that bad? Your family's trying to kill me!"

"Don't be ridiculous."

"Oh yeah? One aunt tries to run me down with her car. Another one tries to poison me. And your cousins are doing a pretty good job of *boring* me to death."

"Don't be so picky," I said. "I have to put up with them all the time."

He gave me a look that would wither grapes. "Exactly! You *have* to put up with them. I don't. What time does the ferry leave in the morning?"

Uh-oh. Did he mean it?

"Take it easy, Jesse. I'll find you something to eat, okay? And it's not *totally* awful here. You like our camping spot, right? You like your little orange tent?"

He gave me a grudging look, then nodded. "Yeah, I like the tent."

"Good," I said. "Why don't you go on down there? I'll rustle up some food and meet you. I have something interesting to tell you too. Kind of a mystery."

The next twenty minutes were the work of a master planner. By offering to help with the dishes, I managed to smuggle a hunk of cheese and a half package of crackers out of the kitchen. Then, when the twins tried to trap me into a new round of Go Fish, I cleverly avoided them by offering to read Hugo his bedtime story – Dr. Seuss. Finally, I talked Aunt Ivy into finding me a big lantern flashlight. Scooping up the cheese, crackers, flashlight, and a deck of cards, I headed across the meadow.

Jesse was in his tent, sitting on his foamy. He'd calmed down a bit, and when he saw the cheese and crackers, he pounced on them like a starving prisoner.

I told him about the Uncle Archie mystery. He wasn't impressed.

"What mystery?" he said between bites of crackers and cheese. "So Aunt Ivy had nightmares. So Uncle Archie joined the circus. So what?"

Maybe you had to be in the family to under-stand. Maybe you had to be around all those years when Uncle Archie's name was never mentioned. You had to know what it meant when my mom hummed.

I pulled out the cards, and we played a couple games of Crazy Eights, followed by War, then Rummy, then Hearts. No Go Fish.

By the time my mom poked her head in to tell us it was bedtime, we were getting along pretty well – even having a few laughs. Jesse had stopped talking about leaving in the morning. I said goodnight and followed my mom to our tent.

Snuggling into my sleeping bag, I smiled with relief. Jesse would have a terrific camp-out night, and we could start fresh in the morning. From now on, I'd make sure he had a good time. I'd be careful to warn him about anything weird that might be coming up.

I fell asleep within minutes and slept soundly – so soundly that when the horrible noises started in the middle of the night, my mom had to shake me awake.

CHAPTER

"**S**TEVIE, WAKE UP! WHAT'S GOING ON?"
An animal? Or was it two? Some kind of fight was going on – right outside our tent. I heard hissing, then snarling. Also a kind of high-pitched chittering.

I sprang to a sitting position, my heart hammering nearly out of my chest. My mom was sitting bolt upright beside me in the dark, one hand clutching my arm.

From the other tent, I could hear Jesse's panicky voice. "Stevie? Mrs. Diamond? What's that noise?"

A loud squeal, and the next time we took a breath, we had our answer.

"Oh, dear heavens!" cried my mom. "It's a skunk!"

I didn't answer. Couldn't. It was way too late for that.

The smell hit the tent like a giant wave, surging through the walls as if they weren't even there. When it reached my nose, it all but paralyzed me. My eyes watered. My throat stung. My nose burned. Eeeeee-yugg! I tried to breathe – couldn't.

I thought I'd faint. I wished I *would* faint.

"Stevie! Get up!" ordered my mom in frantic tones. She was already on her feet, coughing, sputtering, unzipping the tent door. "Bring your sleeping bag."

Jesse, meanwhile, was out there somewhere, squealing, "Help! Help! Aggh!"

By the time we got outside, the skunk was gone. So was whatever it had been arguing with. But the stink was still there, as strong as ever. Glancing around the moonlit clearing, I spotted Jesse. He was outside his tent but still inside his sleeping bag, clutching the top as he hopped toward us.

"Eeegh! What *is* it?"

"Cub odd!" yelled my mom, holding her nose. "We habb to ko back to ta house."

My mom and I started running, stumbling through the dark, dragging our sleeping bags. Jesse tried to hop along beside us until my mom noticed and made him get out of his bag. We ran a bit farther, then slowed down.

We'd left the smell behind.

"What *was* that?" Jesse demanded again. His sleeping bag was balled up in his arms and, even though it was a warm night, he was shivering in bare feet and pajamas.

"A skunk," said my mom. "Must have gotten in a fight with something. A raccoon maybe."

"What do we do now?" I asked.

My mom sniffed her sleeping bag. "I think the bags are okay. We'll have to find somewhere else to sleep. Let's try Cheryl's camper."

Aunt Cheryl was groggy, and she seemed to have a tough time understanding. Eventually, she told my mom that she had room for one person on a pullout bed.

"I'll take it," said my mom quickly. "Leave the door open for me, will you, Cheryl? Stevie? Jesse? Let's find a place for you two."

We ended up on the living room floor in the house, with cushions under our heads and only a thin carpet between us and the wood floor. I tried the couch, but it was too short and saggy.

"It's only for one night," mumbled my mom, heading back to her foamy pullout. "You'll be asleep before you know it."

Jesse settled down about two arm-lengths away from me, right beside the bookshelf. I could hear him snorting and grunting as he tried to get comfortable.

"Well, Miss Stevie Diamond," he finally said in a sulky voice, "this time you've *really* done it."

"Me!" I said. "What did I do?"

Instead of answering, he sniffed huffily.

This was too much. Did he think I *invited* the skunk?

He shifted around again and let out a few more groans, just to make sure I knew how miserable he was. I heard a thump. Fist hitting floor? Nope, too soft. Head hitting floor.

"If I get a sprained back, it'll be your fault."

Ignore him, I told myself.

But he kept groaning. He kept banging against things. He kept muttering about catching the morning ferry. Finally, I couldn't take it anymore.

"Why don't you go back to your tent and sleep with the skunk?" I said. "You're acting like a skunk yourself. You two should get along just fine!"

"Oh yeah?"

I waited, but he was running out of good insults.

"It takes one to know one, Stevie Diamond," he said finally.

Rolling over, I pressed a cushion against my ear. But there were no more complaints. The living room returned to its dark, peaceful middle-of-the-night state.

As I drifted back to sleep, I wondered what else could possibly go wrong with Jesse's visit.

It didn't take long to find out.

CHAPTER

I WAS IN ONE OF THOSE WEIRD SLEEPS YOU FALL INTO
when you're really uncomfortable – like when
you're stuffed up with a cold or sleeping
sitting up in a car. I'm talking about that strange
dozy half-sleep where you feel every ache in
your body.

What woke me up was a light dancing on the
outsides of my eyelids. Opening one eye, I peered
around. When I realized what it was, I opened the
other eye. Then I opened both eyes really wide.

Someone with a flashlight was moving around
the living room. My mom? Still groggy, I didn't
move or say anything. I just watched the flashlight beam move slowly over to where –

Uh-oh.

A sudden anguished howl pierced the air.

"OWWW! HEY! What the –"

Jesse sounded as peeved as the skunk outside
our tent. The flashlight beam bounced wildly
across the living room walls. Shimmying out of my
sleeping bag, I ran for the light switch.

Flick.

Uncle Archie and I stared at each other, open-mouthed, across the room. He was wearing striped pajamas and a plaid grandpa-type housecoat, and his flashlight was now aimed straight at me. I don't know which of us was more surprised. I *do* know that neither of us was as surprised as Jesse, who was sitting on the floor, clutching his foot through his sleeping bag – and yowling.

Uncle Archie had *stepped* on him.

Terrific.

He – Uncle Archie – figured out what had happened about the same time I did. Bending over, he asked Jesse if he was hurt and, if so, where and would he maybe like some ice? He also suggested that Jesse might want to stop making *quite* so much noise unless he wanted to wake up the whole house and everybody in the meadow too.

Jesse stopped yelling. He blinked at Uncle Archie, confused. If you want my opinion, he was only just beginning to wake up. Pulling both legs out of the sleeping bag, he checked his right foot, twisting it in different directions and rubbing the ankle.

"I guess I'm okay," he said finally.

"Are you sure?" asked Uncle Archie. "There's ice in the freezer."

"Nope." Jesse stuck his feet back into the bag and burrowed down inside. "I'm fine."

That's when it occurred to Uncle Archie to ask what Jesse and I were doing there, lying on the floor. I explained about the skunk.

"So your mother's here somewhere too?" Uncle Archie looked around as if he expected my mom to materialize from behind the couch.

"No, she's with Aunt Cheryl."

"Oh," said Uncle Archie. "Well, I'm glad. Glad we didn't wake her, that is. And the others too." He glanced up at the ceiling. We all listened, but there was no sound from the second floor.

Suddenly it occurred to me to ask Uncle Archie what *he* was doing – creeping around in the middle of the night with a flashlight.

"Nothing important. I was having trouble sleeping – old age, I suppose. I thought I'd make myself some warm milk. I had no idea people were camping in the living room." He laughed. "Sorry to disturb you kids. Go back to sleep."

Nodding goodnight, Uncle Archie padded upstairs.

"What time is it?" asked Jesse.

I looked at my watch. "Exactly 4:43."

He groaned and threw one arm over his eyes. "Turn out the light, Stevie."

Seconds later, the living room was dark again and, except for our breathing, silent. I lay on my back, staring up. It must have been getting close to dawn because I could almost see the wiggly crack that runs across the ceiling. I closed my eyes, then opened them again as a question flitted across my mind. Why the flashlight? Uncle Archie didn't know Jesse and I were on the living room floor. Why didn't he just turn on the light? The crack in the ceiling got clearer as I thought about this.

"Stevie? You awake?" Jesse's voice from the bookshelf.

"Uh-huh."

"I can't sleep."

"Me neither," I said. "I guess we've been woken up too many times."

"Do you want to turn the light on? Find something to read?"

"Sure," I said, "but don't blame me if you can't find anything good. Most of the books here are older than my mother."

A sleeping bag rustled. Then a lamp flickered on, and Jesse stood there, rubbing his eyes and looking rumpled. I joined him at the bookcase.

He scanned a row of drab-colored books. "Boy, you weren't kidding. Listen to these titles. *A Naval History of the First World War. Chrysanthemum Cultivation for the Amateur Gardener.*"

"Told you so."

"There's got to be something! Hand me that chair, will you?"

Setting it in front of the bookcase, he climbed up and began to search the high shelves. I checked the low ones. *How to Construct a Compost Box. Sir Winston Churchill: His Complete Speeches. The Care and Feeding of African Violets.*

"Hey!" said Jesse. "Up here."

"What?"

"Some kids' books. Not exactly up-to-date, but better than this other stuff."

I fetched another wooden chair and joined him.

"Look here." He pointed at the titles on the

spines. *"Roger Rover, Boy Explorer. Girl of the Limberlost. What Katy Did."*

The books he was pointing at, like most of the others in the case, were hardcovers, in dull faded colors. Dark blue, dark brown, gray. I glanced through the titles, looking for familiar ones.

"Here's *Little Women*," I said, "and *Anne of Green Gables*."

Jesse frowned. "No offence, but right now I feel like reading about a boy." He flicked a finger at the boy explorer book. "Not this one, though. Can't take a guy named Roger Rover seriously."

I skimmed the titles, pulled out a book and handed it to him. "How about this one?"

He glanced at the cover. *"The Adventures of Tom Sawyer.* What's it about?"

I shrugged. "Some boy who has adventures."

"It'll do," said Jesse. "Have you got one?"

I plucked a book out of the row. "I'm going to find out what Katy did."

I had already put the chairs away and was heading for my sleeping bag when Jesse beckoned me over.

"Hey, Stevie, look at this – inside the back cover of my book. It's a map."

I wandered over, expecting to see a map of Tom Sawyer's adventures. But it wasn't a part-of-the-book map. It was a map somebody had drawn onto the final blank page with an ink pen. There were a few blotchy spots where the ink had smeared and dried, and one corner of the page was torn off at the bottom. I took a closer look.

"I think – yes! It's Catriola Island. See? It's

shaped like a snail." I'd seen this shape on bigger maps of the Gulf Islands. It was how you picked out Catriola Island.

"And this –" I pointed. "This is the aunts' property. See?" The mapmaker had outlined the property in ink. "And here's the ridge that crosses the island, and down below is the pasture where the Smithfields keep their sheep, and here's – what's that?"

I pointed at an "X" on the map. Something was written on it in tiny, pinchy writing. Jesse brought his face closer until it was a nose length away from the page. "It says ... uh ... something cave. It's ... yes, it's ... Rat Cave!"

Sitting up straight, he frowned. "Rat Cave?"

"Ugh!" I said. "I've never heard of anything like that on Catriola. Let me look."

I held the book close to my face and squinted. "It's not Rat Cave. It's *Bat* Cave! That's a B."

"Are you sure?" Jesse took another look. "You're right. Bat Cave. Hey, isn't that where Batman lives?"

"Sure, Jesse. Batman lives on Catriola Island. So does Robin. It's in all the tourist brochures."

"Well, I didn't mean –"

"Never mind. What's this bit?" I pointed at some more tiny writing, just above the torn-off corner. Screwing up my eyes again, I read, "18 – no, 16 – steps s. of arb –"

Jesse frowned. "What's that mean?"

I looked again. "Well, 'S' on a map usually means south. So it's sixteen steps south of arb. But what's an arb?"

Jesse pointed at the corner. "It's torn off there, Stevie. Looks like 'arb' is part of something longer."

I nodded. "But what?"

Suddenly, staring at that map, I had a brainwave. Here it was – the solution to all my problems! A way to keep Jesse from going back to Vancouver. A way to hide from the twins and the Never-Ending Fish Game. Maybe even a way to get some food that wasn't cooked by Aunt Edna.

"Jesse!" I said. "Listen to me."

"I'm sitting right beside you, Stevie, in total silence. What is it?"

"We're going exploring."

"We are?" His eyes lit up. "When?"

"Tomorrow." I glanced out the window, where streaks of dawn were already lighting up the sky. "I mean, today. We're going on an expedition to hunt for Bat Cave. Just you and me. No cousins. We'll leave early – soon, before anyone's up. We'll take the map and – and a picnic lunch."

I waited nervously. How would this offer stack up against a skunk attack, a stepped-on ankle and a lump of gristly meat?

"Great idea!" Jesse pounded his right fist into his left palm. "It'll be almost like a treasure hunt, right? Except, instead of treasure, there'll be –"

He stopped. Frowned. Uh-oh.

"Bats?" he said.

I shook my head quickly. I couldn't lose him. Not now. Not when I was so close.

"It's just a name, Jesse. It doesn't mean a thing."

"It doesn't?"

"Of course not. Think of – well, think of Lake Superior. Just because it's called that, it doesn't mean it's really superior. Right?"

Jesse thought for a moment. "I've never been to Lake Superior."

"Well, I have, and believe me, there's nothing superior about it. And what about New York?"

"What about it?"

"Is it new?"

Jesse's eyes flickered with excitement. "There's nothing new about it," he said. "It's old! I see what you mean, Stevie. You're right."

"Of course I'm right."

Whew!

"But, Stevie?"

"Yeah?"

"What if you're wrong? I mean, what if there actually are bats at Bat Cave? If you think skunks are bad, well, I've heard stuff about bats that would make your skin crawl." His voice got all breathless as he blurted out the details. "Like they're blind, and they can fly into your hair and get all tangled up in it. Some of them are vampires too, with these sharp little teeth that they bite you with. We could end up lying on the cave floor, all pale and bloodless and weak."

He looked pale and bloodless and weak just thinking about it.

Vampires? Hair attacks? Was that stuff true? I glanced over at the encyclopedias, knowing the answer was there – probably in Volume 2. But I couldn't take a chance. If we looked up bats and found out that they actually were blood-drinking, hair-tangling vampires, Jesse would be off this island before you could say "Dracula sucks." No. Better to bluff it out.

"Those are just stories, Jesse. People make stuff up."

He gave me an anxious glance. "You think so?"

I nodded. "Anyhow, you don't have to go inside if you don't want to. We can find the cave first and *then* decide."

He brightened. "Sure. We can decide later. Or we can go in just a little way. Just a few steps." He took a few little shuffling steps toward the kitchen to show me what he meant.

I took a few little copycat steps to show him we were on the same wavelength. Then I took some normal steps, heading for the kitchen.

"I'll hunt up some food," I said over my shoulder. "Why don't you get dressed?"

I opened the fridge and looked around for breakfast stuff. The aunts wouldn't mind. At least, Aunt Ivy wouldn't. She was always telling me to help myself.

A whisper from the living room interrupted my thoughts. Jesse? But who was he whispering to? I tiptoed over and took a peek. There he was, standing in front of the full-length mirror with his hands on his waist and his chest stuck out.

"Jesse Kulniki, Boy Explorer!" he was telling his reflection. Then, a second later, in a slightly louder whisper, "The Adventures of – Jesse Kulniki, Boy Explorer!"

I eased my head back into the kitchen and quietly shut the door.

Mission accomplished.

CHAPTER

I MADE TOAST. THE BREAD WAS THAT HEAVY, HEALTHY kind with five different types of lumpy grains poking out. The peanut butter was the no-salt, no-sugar, no-anything-but-peanuts kind. But Jesse was happy with it, and if he was happy, so was I.

After breakfast, I packed some bread for lunch and found a hunk of cheddar cheese to go with it. A bowl of tomatoes on the counter looked good, and so did a bowl of pears and bananas. After scrounging a small paring knife for slicing and a plastic bottle for water, I tossed the whole works into a plastic bag. As a final thought, I threw in four Edna-cookies. They were a couple of days old, and you'd need a hammer to crack them, but they were as close as we could get to dessert. Maybe Jesse's jaws were stronger than mine.

When we were both dressed, with the lunch and *Tom Sawyer* stowed in a backpack, we stopped by Aunt Cheryl's camper. Creeping in, I woke my mom up – just a little.

"Whu – ?" she mumbled, her eyes half shut.

"Jesse and I are going for a hike on the ridge," I told her. "We'll be back after lunch. Okay?"

She was silent for so long, I thought she'd fallen asleep again. "S'okay," she finally mumbled. "Doan get loss."

"We won't." It would be almost impossible to get lost on Catriola Island. For one thing, it's so small. For another, if you keep walking in any direction, you eventually hit the ocean, along with the road that runs beside it.

It was one of those perfect summer mornings when it's crazy to be anywhere except outside. The meadow was bright with sunshine and dew, and a warm breeze rustled the flowers, stirring up sweet smells. I led Jesse across the meadow and past the orchard to a path leading into the woods. The path started rising right away, but at first it wasn't steep. The trees here were thin, leafy alders. Before long, though, we were walking among the giants of the Catriola forest – huge cedars and firs growing so high, you couldn't even see the tops. They shaded everything underneath, making the trail cool, dark and damp. A few rays of sun fought their way down and made speckled patterns on the ferns.

Jesse and I followed the slowly rising path, stepping around the mucky spots and pushing aside branches. Things were a little overgrown. A club of local hikers had the aunts' permission to use this trail, and they tried to keep it clear, but plants grow really fast around here.

The path began to rise more steeply. As we got closer to the ridge, we had to lean forward. By the time we reached the top, we were puffing a little.

Up on the ridge, we followed the path across a treed area and then came out into the open. The path veered off to our left, continuing along the top of the ridge, but Jesse and I stopped in our tracks.

"Wow!" said Jesse.

I was thinking the same thing.

You could see forever. Well, almost forever. At least as far as Vancouver – a spread-out mass of hazy buildings in the shadow of the tall mountain range behind it. In another direction, you could see Mount Baker, looming out of the clouds – high enough to be snowcapped even in summer. In between was the ocean, or at least the Strait of Georgia part of it, with its dotting of islands.

Far below us, on Catriola, grassy fields were broken up by a few houses and some farm buildings.

"What are those?" Jesse pointed at some whitish bumps in the fields.

"Sheep," I said. "The Smithfields' farm. It's the only big flat area on the island."

Between us and the sheep was a wild rough slope – with Bat Cave somewhere in the middle. It was rocky and uneven, covered in small trees and tangled undergrowth. In some places, it was steep. In other parts, the slope was gentle. Nowhere was there any sign of a path.

"Can you get the map out, Jesse?"

"What? You mean we're already there?" He glanced around eagerly, as if he expected to see the cave entrance a few steps away, or maybe a sign that read "Bat Cave This Way."

"Not exactly." I pointed. "It's somewhere … down there."

Jesse stepped to the edge of the ridge and peered over. The drop was ankle-breaking. "You're kidding, right?"

I shook my head. Reaching into his backpack, I pulled out *Tom Sawyer* and opened it to the map.

"We're right here, on this ridge. And there's the 'X,' so the cave has to be somewhere in the middle of this slope. But we don't have to head straight down from here. Look! It's not as steep over there."

I led him to a place where the slope was more gradual.

"Okay," I said, looking nervously at the area below, "this is it."

"Wait!" said Jesse. "What about the arb? You know – the part about the cave being sixteen steps south of the arb?" He pointed at the tiny writing in the corner of the page.

I nodded. "But we have no idea what an arb is."

"Well, we can at least look for it, can't we?" Jesse waved an arm at the land falling away below. "You're the island expert. Does anything out there look like an arb?"

I scanned the slope. Arb … arb … arb …

Rocks. Salal bushes. Big boulder. Pine tree. Another big boulder. Huge sawed-off cedar tree trunk with new tree growing out of the middle. Oak tree. More salal. Falling-over dead tree. Another boulder. Arbutus tree. Salmonberry bushes …

"Arbutus tree!" I yelled. "There it is, Jesse – the arb. The twisty-looking tree with the peeling red bark and shiny greeny leaves."

"I see it, " said Jesse. "There's only one, right?"

My eyes flickered across the slope. "Yeah, it's the only one. Let's get down there."

From our new spot on the ridge, the route wasn't steep, but in a couple of places, it was grown over with salal – that thick green stuff they use for dead people's wreaths. The sun was higher now and getting hotter. Clouds of insects rose from the bushes and whined in our faces.

Finally we reached the arbutus tree.

"Okay," said Jesse. "Here we are – at the arb. We should be able to see the cave from here, right? If it's only sixteen steps away?"

We turned together in a complete circle. Logs. Boulders. Scrubby growth. No caves.

"Aw, crumb," said Jesse, his shoulders sagging. "After all that work."

I was disappointed too, but I wasn't ready to give up. Not yet. "Why don't we just *try* walking sixteen steps south. Okay?"

He slapped at a gnat-type insect that had landed on his upper lip. "Which way is south?"

That was easy. I looked across the water at Vancouver. The mountains are on the north side of the city. Turning in the opposite direction, I pointed and said, "That way."

"Here goes nothing," said Jesse. He swung in the direction I'd pointed and started marching through the greenery. "One … two … three …"

More salal. A couple of fallen trees. I kept my eyes on my feet as we pushed forward.

Jesse was still counting out steps. "Eleven ... twelve – no cave, Stevie – thirteen ... fourteen ... AAAAAAAEEEIIIII!"

The scream scared me so much that I stumbled, lurching onto my hands and knees. I glanced around frantically.

Jesse was gone!

"Jesse?" I called out in a voice so weak it would have embarrassed a kitten.

Silence.

I tried again, a yell this time. "JESSE?"

A voice came back. Distant. Muffled.

"Down here, Stevie. I fell in a hole."

I gazed around the dense tangled greenery.

"Here!" came the voice. "Over here!"

I followed the sound as Jesse called out again. Walking carefully, I took three steps forward. Then I pushed the bushes aside and looked down.

There *was* a hole! More like a crevice actually – a crack in the ground, about twice Jesse's height, with a couple of huge rocks at the bottom. Jesse was lying beside one of them, staring up. His face was pale and scared-looking.

"Are you okay?" I asked.

He nodded. "I didn't really fall. Just slid down the side."

"You're lucky," I said. It was a long way down, and one of the rocks had a really sharp point.

Jesse's voice was shaky. "I know."

"I'll help you out," I said.

"No. Wait. This is it, Stevie. The cave!"

"This?" I looked around. You'd have to have a pretty good imagination to call this crevice a cave.

"No." Jesse pointed. "Over there. Behind that boulder. There's another hole in the side of *this* hole."

"Stay there. I'm coming down."

By the time I had scrambled down the side, Jesse was on his feet. We stepped around the boulder, and there it was. A thin opening in the side of the crevice – about as tall as me and a little wider.

The entrance to the cave.

"It's real!" I said. "You found it. Excellent work, Jesse. Let's go inside."

"Inside?" Jesse peered through the crack into the darkness beyond.

"Sure." I took a few little steps toward the cave to show him.

"Okay. I just need a minute to ... er ... find this!" He reached into a pocket of his backpack and pulled out a pocket flashlight.

"Brilliant!" I cried. I meant it too. Sometimes Jesse drives me nuts with his fussing. But at times like this, fussing paid off.

He straightened up to his full height – half a head shorter than me – and clicked the light on. "I'll go first," he said. "Just in case there's anything dangerous inside."

Jesse Kulniki, Boy Explorer, speaking. But I couldn't help noticing that his voice was a little wobbly. And his steps toward the cave weren't exactly huge.

Neither were mine, if you want the truth. The word "dangerous" had gotten me thinking about all the things that *could* be inside a cave. A bear, for instance. A cougar. A bottomless pit. A skeleton. A half-crazed hermit with red-rimmed eyes and clawlike hands who –

Stop it, I told myself. Right now.

"Not too fast," I told Jesse as he edged slowly through the opening.

"Don't worry about *that*," he muttered.

Inside, it was as dark as … well, as a cave. Cool too, after the heat of the slope, and damp. I grabbed one of Jesse's hands – just so we'd stay together, of course. He used his other hand to shine the flashlight around the cave walls. They were made of stone and sort of ripply, with hollows, bumps and cracks on the surface. We were inside a cavern about as wide as a living room and twice as long. From what I could tell, it was empty. Jesse shone the flashlight up to an uneven "ceiling" high above our heads.

"See?" I tried to sound cheerful, but my voice echoed, hollow and gloomy, off the stone walls. "Nothing to it."

Jesse didn't answer. Too busy checking things out with his flashlight. The beam was small and not very strong, but it picked out a dark spot at the far end of the cavern. A passage?

"I think this cave goes farther." Jesse sounded like the guy who opens the castle door in Dracula movies.

"Let's take a look." I gave him a little push, and we shuffled toward the dark spot. It *was* a passage. Maybe it led to another section of the cave. I was still holding Jesse's hand when we reached the passage entrance. He shone his flashlight inside, and we were just about to go in when we heard it.

Fluttering.

Jesse let out a low moan.

The fluttering got louder. It was off to the left, to one side of the passage. It was definitely the sound of … wings!

Pain seared my left hand. Jesse was crushing it!

"Ow! Let go!" I said.

He did. The next sound was his running shoes hitting the stone floor as he charged for the exit. He may have taken baby steps on the way in, but on the way out, he was Jesse the Giant.

"Don't take the flashlight!" I yelled.

Too late.

I stumbled through the dark after him.

Outside in the crevice, it was far from bright, but compared to the cave, it was a sundeck.

"Jesse? You okay?"

He was sitting on a boulder, breathing heavily. His thin legs were trembling, especially around the knees. The whites of his eyes were enormous.

He gulped a few more breaths, then spat out a single word. "Bats!"

"Did you see them?"

He shuddered. "Who needed to see them? They were all around us! Fuzzy little wings, sharp teeth, ready to swoop down and –"

I held up a hand. "Wait a minute! I was there too, remember?"

He nodded.

"I didn't *see* a thing," I told him. "That fluttering

sound could have been anything. Let's go back inside."

"Go back? In there? Are you out of your mind? Stevie, the place is called Bat Cave! It says so right on the map. What do you *think* was doing the fluttering? A giant canary?"

This wasn't the right time to laugh, but the image of a huge yellow bird droning around inside the cave was too much for me. I let out a snicker.

Jesse gave me a hurt look.

"Listen," I said, straightening out my face, "even if there are bats, and even if they do get tangled up in people's hair, *you're* not in much danger."

I pointed at his brown hair – clipped short, close to his head. Then I pointed at my own thick mass of curls. "If you were a bat, which one of us would *you* go after?"

"Nice try, Stevie." He shook his head. "I'm still not going back in there."

I shrugged. "Well … I guess … I'll have to go myself."

I waited for him to say it. Oh-I-couldn't-possibly-let-you-do-that.

He held out the little flashlight. "Good luck!"

Entering the cave again, alone, I took even smaller steps than before. Now that I had no one to talk to or hold on to, the cave seemed a lot bigger. I held my breath. Sure enough, when I got to the same place – close to the passage – I heard the fluttering again. And something else. Sort of like … squeaks?

Oh boy.

Feeling silly, I put one arm over my head, covering maybe a tenth of my curly hair. Then I pointed the flashlight straight up, looking for signs of bat life. Scrunched-up wings, bright little eyes, oversized ears ... vampire teeth?

Stop it, I told myself.

No bats. Nothing but the same uneven rock ceiling. I moved the flashlight slowly around the walls, searching. No bats anywhere.

So where was the strange fluttering coming from? Could bats be invisible? Ghost bats, maybe? What if they were the ghosts of bats from some other time, bats that had died violent deaths and were now haunting the cave, seeking new victims for –

Stop it!

"I'm not scared." I said it out loud to the darkness. Then, in a stronger voice, "I'M NOT SCARED."

A new flutter answered me.

Ignore it, I told myself. I headed toward the passage. I hadn't taken more than three steps when something got caught on my foot.

Something soft. Something floppy. I did a little jump, trying to step over it, but it seemed to have wrapped itself *around* my foot.

Okay. Enough bravery.

"YAAHHH!" I screeched. "Get it off me! Off! Get it away!"

Anyone watching would think I'd been stung by a bee. I started doing this wild hopping dance around the cavern, kicking out with both feet, jerking my arms. Something flew across the floor with a soft brushing sound. I stopped, turned and shone my flashlight in the direction of the sound. If it was a dead bat, I'd die. I'd just die. Jesse would have to get a stretcher to carry me out.

It wasn't a bat.

It was a hat! One of those old-fashioned ones that men wear in old movies – the kind with a band and a wide brim. I picked up the edge of it with two fingers, slowly and carefully. I wanted to be absolutely sure there was no dead bat underneath.

No bat.

I scooped up the hat and beamed the flashlight in a circle, trying not to think about the head the hat belonged to. Was *that* somewhere in this cave too? The light traveled across the floor in pale, swirly circles.

No head. No body either.

So here's where I made a choice. I *could* have gone on to the next part of the cave. I probably should have. The passage was right there in front of me. But the hat had finished me off. I felt weak … drained. Jesse's flashlight was looking a little drained too. Its beam was definitely dimmer. I turned it off and on again, but that didn't help.

Pointing the light toward the cave exit, I started walking.

Jesse was sitting on the same boulder, arms wrapped around his knees. When he saw me, he leaped up. "Find anything?"

I held out the hat. It was a dull green color. The brown leather band had a small brown feather in it.

It was pretty dusty, but otherwise good as new.

"Great hat!" said Jesse, running his finger admiringly along the brim. "It's the kind Indiana Jones wears in the movies."

A thought hit me. "You know *why* he wears it?"

"No. Why?"

"To keep off bats."

Jesse rolled his eyes. "No he doesn't!"

"Well, he could. It's a perfect anti-bat hat." I plunked it on his head. "See? It covers your whole head. Hair too. No bat would ever get through that, Jesse. You can wear it when we explore the rest of the cave."

Lifting one hand to the brim, he gave me a wary look.

"Relax," I said. "I don't mean now. The flashlight's almost dead, anyway. Let's eat."

Jesse showed me where he had slid into the crevice – a sandy slope that we now used to climb out. Not far away was a soft mossy spot to sit. Maybe it was the air, or maybe the view – I don't know – but the cheese and tomato sandwiches tasted fantastic, and the pears were the best I'd ever eaten.

When they were all gone, I tried an Edna-cookie. I was right. No way you could bite through it with ordinary human teeth. What you *could* do was gnaw on it till it turned to mush, the way a dog does with a biscuit. I ate two that way.

The hat was still on Jesse's head, shading his face. The brim was tilted low over one eye, and – I had to admit – it did give him an Indiana Jones look. Kind of daring. A bit reckless.

I wasn't going to tell *Jesse* that, of course. He'd never take it off again as long as he lived.

He threw me a lopsided grin. "What are you staring at?"

"The hat. It looks good on you."

He adjusted the tilt. "You think so?"

He took it off and carefully smoothed the brim, brushing a bit of dust from the top. Then he peered inside. "Hey, Stevie, there are initials in here."

He held it up so I could see. Printed in pen on the inside lining of the brim were the letters "O.F."

"O.F.," said Jesse. "What do you suppose that stands for?"

I thought for a moment. "Otto Frankenstein?"

Jesse laughed. "Ozzie Finnegan?"

"Oscar Flugelman?"

We made up more O.F. names on the walk back. It was mostly downhill and easier going. As we followed the path out of the woods and into the aunts' orchard, I was in a good mood. Jesse looked cheerful too, bouncing along on his toes. The cave hunt had been a success – he hadn't said a word all morning about going back to Vancouver.

My mom and Aunty Cheryl were playing badminton on the lawn. Aunty Patricia was playing a baby version of soccer with Hugo. After giving them a ten-second report on our hike – one that didn't include the cave – Jesse and I headed into the kitchen. Aunt Ivy and Uncle Archie were at the sink doing dishes, both of them done up in big flowery aprons. Aunt Edna sat in a wicker chair, her back ruler-straight, squinting at a thick brown book. Over at the kitchen table, Natalie was trapped in a Go Fish game with the twins. Her face had the kind of expression you might get after someone's been twisting your toe for an hour.

I peered into the bowls on the counter on the off chance there was something good to eat.

CRASH!

I whirled around. Bits of broken china skittered across the tiled floor. Aunt Ivy stood clutching her tea towel, frozen like a deer in a car's headlights. She didn't even glance down at the mess she'd made. She was staring at Jesse. From the expression on her face, you'd think he'd grown a second nose.

Jesse looked totally baffled. His eyes traveled to me and then to Uncle Archie, a big question in them. What was going on? Uncle Archie looked as surprised as Jesse and me.

"For pity's sake, Ivy." Aunt Edna heaved herself out of the wicker chair and started picking her way over the broken crockery. "Don't stand there gawking. The broom closet's right behind —"

At that moment, *she* caught sight of Jesse. First she squinted. Then she let out a little cry. Her left hand rose slowly to cover her mouth. Her eyes rolled back in her head, and she started to sway. Then she fell.

Fortunately, Uncle Archie was quick on his feet. He managed to catch Aunt Edna before she hit the ground — just barely. Aunt Edna, being not exactly dainty, did a pretty good job of squashing him flat. Jesse and I ran to help, with Natalie and the twins right behind. Aunt Ivy finally unfroze herself too.

"Oh my! Oh … Edna, are you all right? Archie, are you hurt? Here, Stevie – let's get her into the living room."

Before we could move, my mom and Aunt Cheryl came strolling in, laughing and swinging their rackets. When they saw Aunt Edna out cold on the floor, with Uncle Archie squished underneath and broken china scattered everywhere, they went a little crazy – dropping rackets, yelling questions and grabbing for various parts of Aunt Edna. Aunt Cheryl started taking her pulse.

"She's all right," insisted Aunt Ivy, who had a hold of one of Aunt Edna's ankles and was pulling her toward the living room. "She just fainted, that's all."

It was pretty confused for a while, with everyone talking at once and trying to haul Aunt Edna in different directions. Eventually, we dragged her into the living room and laid her on the couch. Then Jesse and I backed away into a corner, leaving Aunt Edna surrounded by a crowd of chattering relatives.

"What was *that* all about?" Jesse whispered in my ear.

"Beats me," I whispered back. "Ivy and Edna were staring at you."

Worry lines wrinkled Jesse's forehead. "I know. What did I *do,* Stevie?"

I shrugged. "Nothing! It wasn't your fault."

Aunt Edna was trying to sit up now, sputtering and complaining. "I got out of my chair too fast, that's all. It made me dizzy. Why are you making such a fuss?"

Sinking onto the couch beside Edna, Aunt Ivy put an arm around her sister. "Edna's fine," she said. "It was my fault for startling her when I dropped that dish. Silly me. I saw a ... a rabbit out in the garden, and it gave me a start."

A rabbit? Jesse and I exchanged glances. He looked as confused as I felt. Taking off his hat, he scratched his head.

That's when I got it.

The aunts weren't staring at Jesse. They were staring at his *hat!* It was the hat that made Aunt Ivy drop the plate. It was the hat that made Aunt Edna faint.

It was a perfectly ordinary old green hat. Why were the aunts so upset about it? So upset they wouldn't even admit they *were* upset. So upset they'd lie about it.

Rabbit in the garden, my eye.

Something very strange was going on here.

CHAPTER

BEFORE JESSE AND I HAD A CHANCE TO TALK, MY mom cornered us.

"Can you two help out?" she asked in a worried voice. "Cheryl's cleaned up the broken china, and we're trying to convince Edna and Ivy to take a nap. Maybe this reunion is too much for them."

"What do you want us to do?" I asked.

"Tidy up the kitchen? Finish the dishes? Put the kettle on too, will you? I'll make tea."

"No problem," I said. Jesse nodded.

There was no dishwasher, so we had to sort out the washing and rinsing and drying and putting away. When Kevin and Kenneth wandered through, I grabbed them and stuck tea towels in their hands.

"Want to play Dry Dishes?"

To my surprise, they nodded and headed for the sink. Within twenty minutes, we had the dishes all cleaned and put away.

Then I waited for it. It didn't take long.

"Want to play Go Fish?" asked a twin.

"No thanks," I said with a polite smile. "But Natalie's looking for something to do. She's in the living room."

The twins were gone like a shot. Jesse started picking up some newspapers that had been knocked to the floor in all the excitement.

He grinned. "Hey, Stevie! Look at this."

I peered over his shoulder. He was holding a small paperback book. The picture on the cover showed a tall, tanned, black-haired guy in a torn white shirt that showed his rippling muscles. He was clutching a woman with long blonde hair, bright red lips and a low-cut blue dress. The two of them were standing on a balcony at night, staring into each other's eyes. It looked as if they were going to kiss – or maybe smack – each other. Hard to tell from the picture. The title of the book was *Love Beneath the Stars*. Just above the title were the words "Moonlit Romances."

"Who's reading *that?*" I asked. "Natalie?" Had to be.

"No," said Jesse with a giggle. "Aunt Edna. I saw it drop out of the other book she was holding. This one!" He held up the brown book I'd seen Edna reading. *Pruning Your Fruit Trees: A Step-by-Step Guide*.

I gasped. "Are you serious? Aunt Edna? Reading a romance?"

Grinning, Jesse nodded. "She was hiding it between the pages of this pruning book, so nobody would know she was reading it."

"Unbelievable!" I gawked at the book. If you were trying to describe Aunt Edna, "romantic" was the *last* word you'd use.

There was a knock at the kitchen door, and Hank Dooley stuck his head in. He was holding a long skinny parcel wrapped in newspaper. A couple of fish heads poked out the top. I introduced him to Jesse.

Hank nodded and held up the fish. "Caught a couple of cod this morning. They're way too much for me. I wondered if Edna and Ivy could use them – with this big crowd of company and all."

"Sure," I said. "Come on in. I'll call Aunt Ivy."

He stepped through the door. Stopped. Stared. His mustache quivered, and his eyes got as big and round as dollar coins.

I followed his stare to ... the hat! It sat on the kitchen chair, where Jesse had dropped it when we started the dishes.

Hank too? What *was* it about that hat?

Still staring, Hank gave this strange little shiver. Then he rushed over to the counter and dumped the fish on it. "Tell Ivy and Edna I came by. Tell them –"

And he was gone, slamming the door behind him.

"At least he didn't faint," I said.

Jesse looked confused.

"Your hat!" I pointed at it. "It's making everybody crazy. Aunt Ivy, Aunt Edna and now Hank. It's –"

"Stevie?" someone whispered.

I looked around. The door to the dining room opened a crack. Frizzy gray hair, bright blue eyes ...

Aunt Ivy's face poked around. She slipped through the door and peered nervously around the kitchen. Seeing that it was only me and Jesse there, she darted over and took both my hands in hers.

"That hat, dear. Where did you find it?"

"Out by the ridge, Aunty Ivy. There was this crevice in the ground, and Jesse −"

She put a finger to her lips, looked around and whispered, "Shhhh."

I waited.

"Did you … find anything … else with it?" she asked.

"No. Nothing. Listen, Aunt Ivy, what's going on here? What's −"

Again she put a finger to her lips. Smiling gently, she said, "It's a very old story, Stevie. Don't ask me any more. It's best to let sleeping dogs lie. And … I'd appreciate it if you wouldn't mention the crevice to anyone else."

Without waiting for an answer, she turned to Jesse. "The hat looks wonderful on you, dear. I'm sorry I startled you earlier."

She was trying to look calm, but her hands gave her away. She kept twisting them in her flowered apron as if she was trying to dry them − only they weren't wet. Her eyes darted nervously around the kitchen, and she spotted the fish. "Did Hank bring these? How nice. We'll have them for dinner."

She gave a funny little nod, took three quick steps to the dining room door and pushed it open. There was a muffled bang as the door hit something.

"Oh! Goodness! Archie! I'm sorry. I didn't know —"

The door opened wider, revealing Uncle Archie. He was standing there rubbing his nose. It looked pretty red and his eyes were kind of watering, but he smiled cheerfully. "I was just coming in to — to make a pot of tea."

Aunty Ivy blinked at him. "There's tea on the dining room table, Archie dear. Valerie just made it. There's a plate of Edna's delicious cookies too. Come along. I'll pour for you."

Giving Jesse and me a weak little smile, Uncle Archie turned away.

Aunt Ivy paused in the doorway and looked back. "It was awfully good of you to clean up, Stevie dear. I wonder if you'd mind doing me another small favor. We've run out of milk. Could you and Jesse nip down to Priddy's Store?"

"Be glad to," I said. I meant it too. Things were getting really strange around here. It would be a relief to get away. Besides, Priddy's had snacks.

We were barely out of the driveway when Jesse turned to face me, hands on hips. "Okay, Stevie, what's going on? Your relatives are acting like lunatics. And what's all this stuff about the hat?"

After Hank's performance in the kitchen, Jesse had stuffed the hat away in the front hall closet. His head was bare now, but he still looked worried.

"You tell me. All I know is that three people — Aunt Ivy, Aunt Edna and Hank — recognized that hat. It scared them."

"But why? It's just a hat."

I shrugged. "It must have something to do with the cave. After all, that's where we found it."

We stood around for a few minutes, waiting for inspiring thoughts. None came. I pointed down Island Drive in the direction of Priddy's Store, and we began walking, facing the traffic.

I started to think out loud. "Aunt Ivy said it was 'a very old story.' And it's an old hat, the kind people wore a long time ago."

Jesse nodded. "And it was the *old* people who recognized it."

"Right! Aunt Cheryl and my mom didn't even notice it. So here's my theory, Jesse. Whatever's bothering Ivy and Edna and Hank must have happened a long time ago."

"Hmmm," said Jesse. "Funny that Uncle Archie didn't recognize the hat. He's an old guy too, but he hardly glanced at it. No fainting or dish-dropping or anything."

I nodded. That was the problem with theories. They made a lot of sense ... until they didn't.

Priddy's Store isn't big, but it carries just about anything anyone would want to buy. It has to. It's the only store on the island. You can buy food there and clothes and drugstore stuff. You can get fishing tackle, furniture, wine and toys. There's a small magazine section, a rack of paperback books, a film-developing machine, a post office and a shelf of rental videos. I headed straight for the ice cream freezer.

"Ready for one of these?" I asked, flipping up the cover and holding up an ice cream bar.

"Try and stop me." Jesse's left arm and most of his head were already inside the freezer.

"Help yourselves, kiddies!" called a voice from the other end of the store. It was Mr. Priddy, the owner, a chubby little guy with a rim of fuzzy gray-brown hair around his head and a matching rim of beard around his chin. He was sitting beside the cash register doing a crossword puzzle. Once, long ago, my mom had introduced me to him, but he never remembered me. "Perfect day for ice cream, wouldn't you say? If you're looking for cold drinks, they're in the other cooler – over by the baked goods."

"Thanks!" I called back.

Mr. Priddy returned to his puzzle. Jesse and I each picked out an ice cream bar. Then we took a plastic jug of milk from the dairy section.

Jesse nodded toward an "Island Announcements" bulletin board beside the fridge. "Look, Stevie. They show movies in the community hall on Friday nights. Will we still be here then?"

I didn't answer. I wasn't listening. Another notice had caught my eye.

"Catriola Island Historical Society," it said. "Meetings second Wednesday of every month at the Community Hall." There was a bunch of information about upcoming meetings, but the interesting line was at the bottom. "For more information, contact Theodore Priddy, President, at Priddy's Store."

I glanced over at the cash register. There he was – right under our noses. The president of the island's historical society. We needed to ask *someone* about the cave and the old hat and the "old story" Aunt Ivy wouldn't tell us. Who better than Mr. Priddy?

But we'd have to do it carefully. If we asked too directly, he might get all nervous, like Aunt Ivy, and start talking about sleeping dogs. We'd have to be subtle. Clever. We'd have to hint at things.

I glanced at Jesse. He was reading more notices as he worked on his mint chocolate ice cream bar. A chocolate smear covered his upper lip. Another splotch decorated his chin.

Maybe I'd better do the questioning myself.

"Let's go pay for this stuff," I suggested. "And Jesse?"

"Uh-huh?"

"For the next few minutes, let *me* do the talking. Okay?"

He nodded agreeably and, still licking, followed me to the cash register. I handed Aunt Ivy's twenty-dollar bill to Mr. Priddy.

"You kids visiting from Vancouver?" Mr. Priddy put down his pencil, stood and turned toward the cash register. "We get lots of Vancouver folks these days, ever since the new lodge opened down the road. In and out of here all day. Mind you, I'm not complaining. Good for business, right? Good for the island."

I nodded, glad to see he was so talkative. "We're just here for a few days. This island's great. So much … history!"

Jesse stopped licking.

Mr. Priddy peered at me. "You interested in history?"

"Oh sure. I mean, what *is* history, after all? It's just stories, right? About the past? I love stories!"

Jesse frowned, his brow wrinkling with confusion.

"You're right!" cried Mr. Priddy. "That's *exactly* what history is. Although, I must say, it's not everyone your age who sees it that way."

I shrugged modestly. "I bet there are a lot of ... you know ... great stories about this island."

I paused. Would he take the hint?

He leaned forward, belly resting against the cash register, and started poking the air with one finger. "I could tell you stories about this island that would make your head spin. There ought to be a book written about this island. If I ever get a few months free –"

"Any stories about caves?" I interrupted.

"Caves?" Mr. Priddy took a step backward. Jesse started coughing, really loud. A warning.

Okay. Maybe I was rushing things.

"We – er – like caves," I said, trying not to sound nervous. "It's kind of a hobby."

"That's right," said Jesse. "We're ... cave-ologists."

Mr. Priddy grinned. "Cave-ologists, you say. Well, I guess a couple of ... cave-ologists deserve a good cave story." He paused and gazed out the window, thinking. We waited.

Suddenly, he snapped his fingers. "I *do* know a cave story."

"You do?" said Jesse.

Mr. Priddy nodded. "It's a real doozy. Part of Catriola history too." Leaning forward, he lowered his voice, as if he was telling us a secret. "It's called … the Legend of Bat Cave!"

My mouth must have dropped open – I noticed that I had to close it. I glanced sideways at Jesse. He was staring, goggle-eyed, at Mr. Priddy. Green ice cream trickled onto his hand.

Mr. Priddy settled back on his stool with a chuckle. I could see he was enjoying this. He nodded toward a couple of stools. "Grab a seat."

We sat.

Mr. Priddy closed his eyes and took a deep breath. Yup, he was enjoying this all right.

"It started," he said, "about a hundred years ago. Catriola Island was a wild place back then. Hardly a soul living here. But it was right on the route to the Klondike Gold Rush. Ships came past here all the time, taking gold hunters up north to the Klondike and bringing them back down again. Most of those fellows were broke and starving on their way back. But a few found gold. Oh yes – a few got rich."

Jesse licked the back of his hand and nodded. "We learned about the Klondike Rush in school."

Mr. Priddy continued as if he hadn't heard a word.

"Well now, back in 1899, one of those ships coming back ran aground – right here, off the coast of Catriola Island. It got caught on a sandbar at low tide, they say, and was stuck for almost two days. During those two days, there was a robbery. One of the prospectors on board had struck it rich and was carrying a sack of gold nuggets. He was smart enough to keep it with him every minute.

But he had to sleep, you see, and when he woke up one morning, it was gone. Stolen!

"Well, normally, when a ship is out at sea, this wouldn't be a problem. The captain would just search the ship and find the gold – and the thief too. And the captain *did* do a search. But the gold wasn't there. Can you guess why not?"

Jesse held up his hand, like in school. "Someone brought it onto the island?"

Mr. Priddy thumped a fist on the counter. "Exactly! In the dead of night, the thief rowed a lifeboat over to the island and hid the gold. Hid it in a cave, they say."

Jesse's head swiveled in my direction. I kept my eyes firmly on Mr. Priddy.

"Afterward, the thief snuck back on board the ship. The rumor is, he was planning to come back later to fetch the gold. But as far as anyone knows, he never did. And for the last century, people on Catriola Island have been talking about that sack of gold nuggets. It's become a legend. The cave has become a legend too. Among us islanders, it's known as Bat Cave."

I took a deep breath. It was time for the million-dollar question.

"Where *is* Bat Cave?" I asked.

Mr. Priddy grinned. "If I knew that, do you think I'd be sitting here? Don't you think I'd be out there in that cave right this minute, gathering up those gold nuggets?" Giving the counter a hearty whack, he let out a wheezy laugh that ended in a cough.

Jesse and I stared at him. Neither of us cracked a smile.

Mr. Priddy stopped laughing. He rubbed his chin. "Here's the truth, kids. There *is* no cave! It's just a story. I know Catriola Island like the back of my hand, and there's not a cave anywhere on it."

"So no one ever found any ... gold nuggets?" Jesse's voice had gone a little squeaky.

Mr. Priddy shook his head. "Never! But rumors about that cave have been floating around this island for a hundred years, causing all kinds of trouble. Tragedy, even. Oh my, yes."

Heaving a loud sigh, he stood up and hit some buttons on the cash register. "That'll be $6.93. You kids need a bag?"

I shook my head. He handed us the milk and our change and picked up his newspaper with the crossword puzzle.

Jesse and I were already at the door when I realized that we weren't finished yet. Nowhere near. I stopped.

"Did he say tragedy?" whispered Jesse.

We turned and headed back to the counter.

"Mr. Priddy?"

He blinked up at me, surprised.

"What did you mean – tragedy?" I asked.

He fiddled with his pencil for a moment, chewing on his lower lip as he thought. "Well," he said finally, "I guess the worst was that business with Orville Frisk."

Orville Frisk.

O.F.!

I glanced at Jesse. He didn't seem to have made the connection.

"That's a whole different story," said Mr. Priddy. "Are you sure you've got time to hear it?"

I nodded so hard my neck hurt. "Tons of time! We love stories. History, you know."

I nudged Jesse onto one of the stools. Climbing onto the other, I nodded at Mr. Priddy to begin.

His gaze drifted, focusing finally on some paper towels on a high shelf. "It was about forty, forty-five years ago, a fellow named Orville Frisk came to Catriola Island. He was a – a what do you call it – a naturalist. One of those fellows who loves nature. He said he was here to study the wildlife – not that we've got much, in my opinion. But this Orville, he started wandering all over the island with his butterfly nets and his bird books and whatnot. You'd see him everywhere. Long, tall beanpole of a guy."

"Did you say he studied birds?" asked Jesse eagerly. "That's really interesting. I –"

I silenced him with a single fierce glare.

"People on the island are friendly to strangers," Mr. Priddy went on. "One family was particularly good to Orville. Took him into their house, fed him – that sort of thing. They were pretty darned unhappy when the truth came out."

Turning to face us, Mr. Priddy paused.

"What truth?" I asked quickly.

"Orville Frisk wasn't a naturalist at all. He was a treasure hunter! He'd heard about the lost Klondike gold, and he was *pretending* to be a nature lover so he could search the island. I suppose he figured that if he found gold on someone's property, he would just grab it and disappear."

"That's not very nice," said Jesse.

Mr. Priddy gave a little snort of agreement. "When the truth came out, there were a couple of young fellows who got pretty mad about it. One of them was from that family I told you about – the one that invited Orville Frisk to stay with them. These two young fellows – best friends, they were – had been guiding Frisk around on his so-called nature walks. When they found out he was lying, they were pretty ticked off. Frisk was searching *their* property on *their* island. If there was any lost Klondike gold – well, they figured they had more right to it than he did."

"Sure they did," said Jesse. "Frisk was a crook."

I leaned forward. "So what happened next?"

"Well, the first thing was – Orville Frisk got chucked out of this family's house. But he was a determined son-of-a-gun, and he didn't give up easily. He put up a tent on the beach and kept searching the island. Can you beat that?"

Jesse let out a grunt. "Pushy!"

"Very pushy," agreed Mr. Priddy. "So those two young fellows, they decided to try to beat Frisk to the gold. After all, *they* knew the island. They were sure they could find the gold first. But then …"

Another pause. A long one. Mr. Priddy's face got all tense and serious. "One fateful night … *something happened.*"

There it was again! My mom's phrase. From the ferry.

"Nobody knows what it was," said Mr. Priddy. "Not for sure. It started at a dance at the community hall. There was an argument between Orville Frisk and one of those young fellows I was telling you about. Half the people on the island heard it. The lad was telling Frisk to stay off his land, and Frisk was saying he'd go wherever he blinking well pleased. Pretty soon one of the ladies in charge of the dance asked them to leave, which they did – together. They were still pushing each other around and arguing."

"And?" I said.

Mr. Priddy gave me a solemn look. It must have lasted a whole minute. Then he let out a sigh. "Orville Frisk was … never … seen … again."

Now it was Jesse's and my turn to stare, speechless.

"Wow!" said Jesse finally. "What happened to him?"

"No one knows." Mr. Priddy shook his head sadly. "His tent stayed right there on the beach. He never went back to it."

My mind raced. "Well, um … maybe he just left the island. Maybe he couldn't be bothered to take his tent."

Mr. Priddy shrugged. "Could be. But nobody *saw* him leave. Back then, we islanders always knew who came and went on the ferry."

Jesse's eyes flickered back and forth as he thought out loud. "Maybe he didn't take the ferry. Maybe he rowed or motored over to another island – in a little boat."

"Could be," said Mr. Priddy again, staring at the ceiling. "But whose boat did he take? He didn't have his own, and none of the island boats went missing."

There was another long pause while we all thought about Orville Frisk and his mysterious disappearance all those years ago.

"So," said Jesse, "nobody has any idea what happened on … that fateful night?"

"Oh, people have their suspicions," said Mr. Priddy. "The young fellow Frisk argued with – well, he disappeared too, the very next day. Took off on the morning ferry like he'd been shot out of a cannon. Come to think of it, he probably *did* get shot out of a few cannons later in his life because – guess what? – he joined the circus!"

Mr. Priddy chortled away, enjoying his own joke. "Went all the way to Europe. Sent postcards home! They came right through our post office here."

He laughed again, but when he realized that *we* weren't laughing, he stopped. Suddenly, his face changed. He leaned across the counter, stared at me hard, especially my hair, and said, "Wait a minute. Aren't you a Cooper? Valerie Cooper's daughter?"

I nodded. "But her name is Diamond now."

"Oh my gosh!" Mr. Priddy looked as if he'd just been slapped. "Me and my big mouth. Listen, kids, all these stories I've been telling you – well, that's all they are. Just stories, you understand. Like you see on TV?"

"Uh, sure," said Jesse uncertainly.

"I told you it was a legend, didn't I?" Mr. Priddy was quickly turning a tomato-ish red. "Lost gold? Bat Cave? What a pile of hooey!"

"Sure," I said.

"And about Orville Frisk? I'm sure you two are right. He must have got off Catriola under his own steam. We just never noticed. So many boats on an island, who'd miss one? Ha ha ha. Now, can I get you anything else before you leave? Potato chips? Chocolate bar? Nice big package of chewing gum?" He was on his feet now, picking up snacks and waving them at us.

"No thanks," I said. "We have everything we need."

Without another word, Jesse and I left the store and walked, double quick, down the highway. A truck with a big brown dog in the back whizzed past. The dog barked when it saw us, but we barely gave it a glance. With every step I took, the plastic jug of milk banged against my left leg. *Slosh, thunk, slosh, thunk.* We didn't slow down until we were around the first curve, out of sight of the store.

Jesse grabbed my arm and pulled me into an area half hidden by scraggly bushes. We collapsed onto the mossy ground.

"Stevie! Did you *get* it? Do you *know* who those two young fellows were?"

"Of course I know." I moved a knobby branch I had landed on. "Archie and Hank! And the one who got into a fight with Orville was Uncle Archie."

Jesse was shaking with excitement. "But don't you know what it *means?* It means your Uncle Archie is a mur –"

I held up a finger. "Don't say it, Jesse! Don't even say the word."

"But the cave! The gold! And Orville Frisk! Mr. Priddy says Frisk was mur −"

This time my hand came down over his mouth, covering it right up. I waited till he'd calmed down a bit. Then I handed him the jug of milk.

"Here. Drink!"

He stared at it. "I don't have a cup. I −"

"Drink!"

He took the jug, unscrewed the top and glugged down a couple of long swallows. Wiping his mouth with the back of his hand, he passed the jug back.

"Thanks," he said. "I needed that."

I took a long swallow myself. Then I put the jug down and leaned forward, elbows on knees.

"First of all, we don't know that Orville Frisk was mur−" Oh what the heck. I said it. "Murdered. All we know is, he disappeared. No body was found. No witnesses. No evidence. This is *not* a murder case. Not yet anyway. It's a missing persons case."

"Missing person?" Jesse snorted. "He's been missing for more than forty years! What do you think? He's been wandering around the island all this time?"

I didn't answer. Jesse's stare was making me really uncomfortable.

"Face it," he said. "The guy's dead. Kaput. Finished."

I started digging at the moss with a twig. "Maybe so. But that doesn't mean Uncle Archie mur − that it was Uncle Archie's fault."

"No," said Jesse with a little shrug. "I suppose it could be just a *coincidence* that Archie had a huge fight with Orville Frisk. It could also be a *coincidence* that Archie was the last person to see Orville Frisk alive – they left the dance together, right? And, oh yeah, there's that other little *coincidence* – that Archie took off like a scared rabbit the very next day."

Hearing him put it so bluntly, I got a little queasy. The milk seemed to be curdling on its way to my stomach.

"Okay," I admitted, "it doesn't look good for Uncle Archie. But think about it. He *did* come back. And he didn't flip out when he saw the hat."

"The hat?" Jesse looked confused. "What's the hat got to do with anything?"

I threw my twig at him. "For Pete's sake, Jesse! The initials written inside? O.F.?"

I waited, but he continued to look at me blankly.

"You were wearing Orville Frisk's hat!"

You know how you read in books sometimes that all the color drains from someone's face? I never really knew what it meant until that moment. Jesse's face slowly changed from pinkish brown to ghost-white. His voice came out halting and jerky.

"That ... was ... Frisk's hat?"

I nodded. "It's why everyone acted so strange today. Nobody's seen that hat in forty-five years. I bet no one's visited the cave either. You've got to admit – it's a pretty hard place to find."

Jesse stared at his running shoes, looking sort of sick. Maybe the milk *he* drank was turning sour too.

"Stevie?" he said after a moment.

"Yeah?"

"How far did you get? In the cave, I mean. You didn't get to the end, did you?"

I shook my head. "I didn't go into the passage."

"So there could actually be … gold nuggets in there. Right?"

The lost Klondike gold. I'd been so busy thinking about Orville Frisk and Uncle Archie, I'd forgotten all about it.

"Sure, there could be gold nuggets." I paused a moment. "There could be *anything* in that cave."

I didn't think it was possible, but Jesse's face got even whiter. Grabbing the jug of milk, I got to my feet. Jesse stood up too, and we pushed our way through the low-slung branches that shielded us from the road.

Out on the highway, I stopped. "You know what we have to do, don't you?"

Jesse gave me a sideways look. "Yes. And I don't like it."

I waited.

He let out a long sigh. "We have to go back to Bat Cave. Right?"

I nodded. The milk in my stomach moved one step closer to cottage cheese.

Bat Cave was waiting.

And there could be … anything … inside.

CHAPTER

"**P**ICK WEEDS? NOW?"

My mom nodded. While we were gone, she and Aunt Cheryl had organized a work party in the garden and orchard. The whole family was invited – in other words, commanded – to join in. Jesse and I were put in charge of weeding. The twins were assigned to help.

"But, Mom, we were just –"

"Everyone's helping, Stevie. Everyone!"

Bat Cave would have to wait. We headed for the garden.

Weeding it was a big job. The aunts grow tons of vegetables so they can freeze them or put them in jars for the winter. Pickled onions, canned pears, corn relish, stewed tomatoes, dilled cucumbers. As I cleared the weeds out of the onion patch, I remembered the year we had visited at harvest time. I didn't know there were that many cucumbers on the planet!

Today, though, with four of us weeding, it wasn't so bad. And it was a great excuse to put off the cave visit. As I yanked and dug, I kept an eye on Uncle Archie, stacking wood over by the shed. Could a sweet grandpa-looking guy like that really be a murderer? A guy who juggled and rode a bike backward? My mother's uncle?

Who could tell?

Not me, that's for sure. I was starting to feel like a pretty poor excuse for a detective. How on earth had I missed the Klondike gold story all these years? And the legend of Bat Cave? And Orville Frisk? I'd been coming to this island since I was a baby. I'd been staying with the aunts, playing with the neighbor kids, talking to Hank. How could this stuff get past me? How could I not notice?

You *deserve* to be picking weeds, I told myself.

But it was hard to keep my mind on the garden. I didn't even notice when one of the twins – Kevin, I think – started pulling up spinach plants. Before I could stop him, he had yanked up a whole row. I told him not to worry. It was only spinach. But there was lots of good stuff in the garden too. Baby carrots, crunchy and sweet. Juicy green peas. Rosy pink raspberries. Strawberries just turning red. Jesse filled a small plastic bag with extra pickings.

"To get me through dinner," he said.

Dinner was Hank's fish. I was hoping it would end up in batter, with fries on the side, and maybe some cole slaw. I should have known better. Aunt Edna had stuck it in a casserole. It got lost in a mush of watery rice, soggy carrots and the spinach that Kevin had pulled up.

"I don't usually put spinach in this casserole,"

95

said Aunt Edna, eyeing Kevin. "But waste not, want not."

"An excellent motto," said Uncle Archie as he spooned some onto his plate. "Who else for seconds? Jesse?"

During dinner, I kept a close eye on the aunts. Were they still rattled from seeing the hat? No, they seemed back to normal – whatever that was. I watched Uncle Archie too, looking for signs of criminality. Shifty eyes? A mean mouth? He looked as grandpa-ish as ever.

When we were finished eating, little Hugo put on a "show." We all sat and watched as he charged around the living room, dressed in a blue tablecloth and growling like a bear. The grown-ups loved it. They clapped as if it were a Broadway hit, and my mom took a whole roll of film. Later, Aunt Ivy got a game of charades going. By the time we went back to our tents, it was after ten o'clock.

"We'll leave for the cave at dawn," I whispered to Jesse as he headed for his tent.

"Dawn," he whispered back.

Outside my own tent, my mom was carefully sniffing the air. "Just making sure that skunk hasn't come back." She shone her flashlight suspiciously around the tent's edges.

"Skunk? Oh yeah." It seemed like a week since the skunk fight. I took a deep breath. The smell was gone.

"Mom?" I said, following her inside.

She was busy sniffing her sleeping bag. "Yes, Stevie?"

"Did you ever hear any stories about lost gold here on the island? Or a place called Bat Cave?"

She laughed. "Where'd you hear those old fairy tales?"

"Mr. Priddy. At the store."

Sticking her face into a pillow, she breathed in, then pulled back and coughed. "Phew! I should have aired this out. Mr. Priddy? Don't believe everything *he* tells you. I've never in my life run into a bigger gossip than Ted Priddy."

More sniffing as she crawled around the tent. They could make a movie. *My Mother, the Bloodhound.*

"How's your sleeping bag, sweetie?" Sniff, sniff, sniff. "Okay?"

"It's fine, Mom."

The skunk didn't show its face – or any other part of itself – that night. At dawn, Jesse woke me up with scratching noises on the outside of my tent. After gulping down a quick breakfast, we headed for the path that led to the ridge.

The morning was as pretty as the day before, but in a different way – full of misty shadows, with little bird sounds coming from the woods. In the distance, a woodpecker rat-a-tatted at some tree. None of it helped the sinking feeling in my stomach, a feeling that got worse with every turn in the path. Each step took us closer to the cave … and whatever was inside.

By the time we reached the ridge, I felt terrible. I felt even worse as we climbed down into the crevice. Now that we knew where the cave was, it was easy to find. The *hard* part was going inside.

I stood outside the cave entrance, trying to work up my courage. Behind me, Jesse was pulling something out of his backpack.

When I saw what it was, I sighed.

"Jesse, *what* are you doing?"

"What? You mean, the hat?" It wasn't the Orville Frisk hat. It was a wool hat, the kind you wear skiing.

"Just a precaution," he explained. He put it on and yanked it down as far as it would go, trying to cover his neck with it.

"Precaution?"

"I figured you were right about a hat being protection against vampire bats. Not that I'm saying there really *are* vampire bats here. It's just a … you know, precaution."

"I don't *belieeeve* this! Vampires? Next thing you know, you'll be carrying around garlic cloves for protection."

Something in his expression gave him away.

"No way! You *did* bring garlic, didn't you? Where is it? In your pocket? For crying out loud, Jesse. Garlic?"

He held up his hands in protest. "We don't know what we're going to find in that cave, Stevie. It's good to be prepared."

Reaching into the backpack, he pulled out the two large flashlights we had borrowed from the aunts' shed. I took one and headed into the cave.

"I don't know what your problem is," I muttered over my shoulder. "A bird lover like you – you'd think you'd *like* bats."

"Bats aren't birds." Jesse's voice echoed off the dark walls. "They're mammals."

"So what? They have wings, don't they?"

"Yes. But bats don't lay eggs, the way birds do. And they have fur instead of feathers and —"

"Jesse?"

"Yeah?"

"We'll do bat study later, okay?"

"Oh. Right. You first."

Sure. Me first.

With the big flashlights, we could see a lot more of the cave. We moved the beams over the stone surfaces as we walked slowly toward the far end. Jesse focused on the right wall. I checked out the left. Dips. Bulges. Shadows. Cracks. Heart.

Heart?

I backed up.

"Look, Jesse."

On a chest-high place on the wall, a heart had been scratched. I shone my flashlight on it. Something had been scratched inside it. I looked closer. It was old and faint. Even up close, I couldn't make it out.

"Weird," I said, running my fingers over the scratching.

"Everything in here is weird," said Jesse. "Can we please hurry?"

He was right. If we didn't keep moving, we'd lose our nerve. We took a few more steps, pointing our flashlights up, down, sideways.

"What's that over there?" Jesse focused his beam on the floor.

Something tiny. I wouldn't even have noticed it if he hadn't pointed it out. We walked over together and crouched down.

"Cigarette butts." Jesse picked one up. "They look old. All shriveled up."

"Bring them along," I told him. "See anything else?"

He reached for my hand. "Stevie? What's that?"

Before I could answer, or see what he'd found, he spoke again. He sounded scared. "Stevie?"

"Yeah?"

"It's bones!"

He was already moving toward the exit, but I hung on to his hand tight. Holding my breath, I shone my flashlight on the place where he'd been looking.

"Jesse, wait! It's okay. They're just little. Like … chicken bones."

"Ch-chicken?"

"Sure. Hey, look! They *are* chicken bones. See? Here's a wishbone!"

I held it out.

"I knew that," he said. "I knew they were chicken bones."

"Good," I said. "Let's keep moving."

We were almost at the passage now.

"Get ready," I said and squeezed his hand.

Just like the day before, a flutter broke the silence – and another and another. Then some of those strange squeaks. Then more flutters – like tiny wings beating all around us. The sound filled the air.

This time we were ready for it. We didn't scream.

We didn't run. Our hands just gripped each other more tightly, and Jesse's got all sweaty. The cold shiver that had been hanging around the bottom of my spine broke loose and wriggled across my back.

I shone my flashlight up. Down. Sideways.

"No bats," I said.

"Good," said Jesse.

He didn't *sound* good.

"Keep going?"

"Uh … yeah."

I shone my flashlight beam ahead until it rested on the dark opening at the end.

The passage.

My stomach did a little flip.

"Stevie?"

"Yeah?"

"Be careful. There could be a big drop … or something."

The passage was long and narrow. It pressed against my shoulders as I squeezed inside. Behind me, Jesse made an unhappy sort of "Unnhhh" noise, and I remembered that he had claustrophobia – fear of closed-in places. Of course, he also had a fear of the dark and a fear of heights and a fear of bats.

Well, maybe it was good for him to face his fears. Maybe.

"You okay, Jesse?"

"Unnhhh."

The rock walls closed in tighter … and tighter still. I could feel them scrape roughly against my shoulders. Cold. Hard. Damp. For one horrible second, it felt like they were … moving inward.

It was crazy – I knew it was crazy – but it felt as if the walls were trying to crush me.

Claustrophobia! Had to be. I stopped. Took a deep breath. *Hnnnnnhhhhh.* Then, stepping forward, I forced my way into –

A second cavern.

This one was so low I had to bend over to walk in it.

With a grunt, Jesse squished in beside me. As I lurched forward, my head scraped the ceiling. I gulped a breath of dank cave air and flashed my light around. Jesse beamed his around too.

Rock walls. Uneven floor. Lumpy ceiling.

"See any gold nuggets?" asked Jesse in a quavery voice.

"Not so far."

Hunched over, we started looking around. The walls here had more cracks and crevices than the first cavern, and we took time to shine our flashlights into each one. How big was a sack of gold nuggets anyway? Where would a thief hide it? I concentrated hard on those nuggets so I wouldn't think about what else might be there.

This cavern was longer than the first. Even so, it only took about five minutes to search it. Empty. Not even cigarette butts or chicken bones.

"Are we done?" asked Jesse. "Good! Let's get *out* of here!"

He didn't have to convince me. We turned back toward the passage. Jesse had one foot inside when suddenly he stopped.

"What's that?" he whispered.

"What?"

"That noise."

All I could hear was his breathing, ragged and rough. And my own heart, of course. *Ba-boom. Ba-boom. Ba-boom.*

"What noise?"

Was he talking about the fluttering?

Then I heard it.

It was coming from the first cavern. It began as a low sigh. Then it got louder ... and louder ... and turned into a moan.

Oooooooooooooooooooooooh.

I froze. The hairs on the back of my neck stood straight up. That wasn't a bat sound. No way.

On the other hand, it wasn't exactly human either.

CHAPTER

JESSE'S HAND REACHED BACK AND GRABBED MINE. His fingers were damp, icy cold. In the stillness of the cave, our breathing was as loud as thunder. *Hhh. Hhh. Hhh.*

We crouched, straining to hear …

Yes. There it was –

Ooooooooooooooooh.

I sucked in my breath. Clutched Jesse's hand tighter.

Goooooooooooooooo.

Go? Was that "go"?

Jesse's nails dug into my skin. My flashlight fell, hit the ground with a thunk. Was that my heart pounding so loud? Or Jesse's? Raspy breathing filled my ear. His? Mine?

Hhh. Hhh. Hhh.

Ba-boom. Ba-boom. Ba-boom.

Another moan.

Hooooooooooooome.

I couldn't move. Every muscle in my body tightened, obeying some don't-move command from inside. Mouth dry. Eyes wide. Waiting …

Ba-boom. Ba-boom. Ba-boom.
Hhh. Hhh. Hhh.
Ba-boom. Ba-boom.

How long did we crouch there? Seconds? Minutes? It wasn't until Jesse's fingers loosened that I realized the moaning had stopped.

"Wh-what *was* it?" Jesse's voice was tiny.

"I don't know ... but I bet you a million bucks it wasn't bats."

It was as if someone had flashed a "go" signal. Jesse pushed forward, grunting. He slithered through the passage like he'd been greased. I picked up my flashlight and, a moment later, popped through behind him into the first cavern. We both flashed our lights around the walls. This was where the sound had come from.

Empty. Silent. No sign of life.

At the far end was ... sunlight!

From just above my head came a flutter. Then another ... and another.

Jesse and I ran so fast we barely touched the ground.

Bursting outside, we scrambled up the side of the crevice. Then, spiderlike, we half ran, half crawled across the tangled growth. When we hit the ridge, we kept going – along the top, down the path, running hard, running fast, until we were deep in the woods again.

Finally, Jesse collapsed against a log. He grabbed his side. "Stop! I'm getting a cramp!"

I spotted a stump and fell onto it. For a long time, we just flopped there, gulping air.

"I know ... what that was," gasped Jesse.

"Whuh?" I gasped back.

Panting every few words, Jesse plunged on. "Before he disappeared … Orville Frisk was … hanging around the cave. We know that … because of the hat. So it makes total sense that … if he died …"

A long pause, filled with heavy breathing.

"… he'd stick close by … his *hat!*"

This was too much, even for someone as scared as me. "He'd stick close to … his hat?"

Jesse glowered. "That's right. His hat! Go ahead and laugh, Stevie, but we both know what was making that noise. The ghost of Orville Frisk! It was warning us to stay away from the cave."

Uh-oh. I was hoping I was wrong. I was hoping Jesse had heard something different in the cave.

So it *wasn't* just moans or noises. It *was* words. But a ghost?

"My mom says there's no such thing as ghosts."

Jesse snorted. "That's only because she's never been trapped in a cave with one. Wait till a ghost tells her to gooooooooooooo hoooooooooooome. She'll change her mind in a hurry."

"Are you sure that's what it said? 'Go home'?"

He nodded. "And as far as *I'm* concerned, it's a great idea."

He stood up and started marching down the path. "It's nice and safe at home," he added over his shoulder.

"Dull too," I mumbled.

"What?"

"Nothing."

I followed him along the trail.

It was a good thing we had such a long walk back. Plenty of time to calm down. After the blackness of the cave, the dark woods seemed almost bright. I was happy to put one foot in front of the other on the solid dirt path and listen to sounds I understood. Birds twittering. Insects buzzing. By the time we came out of the forest, I felt back to normal. Almost.

We could hear laughter long before we reached the house. Out in the yard, Uncle Archie and the twins were tossing scarves in the air.

"Hey, Stevie!" yelled a twin. Kevin, I think. "Uncle Archie's teaching us to juggle. Look!"

He had two scarves in his left hand and one in his right. As I watched, he tossed a scarf in the air with his left hand. It flew up, then slowly floated down, like a parachute. As it fell, he threw the scarf in his right hand into the air and used that hand to catch the falling scarf. Meanwhile, the left hand was throwing the last scarf up and catching the dropping one, and so on.

"See? I'm juggling!" Kevin was grinning. Giggling too. Kevin!

Kenneth was doing the same thing with another set of scarves, and Uncle Archie was using oranges. Hugo had only one scarf, and he was having trouble catching even that. Not that he cared.

"Jugging!" he yelled, hurling the scarf into the air with both hands. "Jugging!"

We headed for the porch, where my mom was taking pictures. "Hi, guys," she said as we climbed the steps. "You missed circus school. Uncle Archie's been showing the twins tricks all morning. I've never seen them so excited. And look at Hugo!"

Letting out a shriek of joy, Hugo plopped onto his backside and watched as his scarf drifted down over his head. The twins were hooting at each other.

"You're sure he's been here the whole time?" I asked my mom. "Uncle Archie?"

She squinted through her lens and clicked. "Since breakfast. Why?"

"Oh … no reason."

No reason, except on the last half of our walk home, I had started to wonder about Uncle Archie and all those fresh-air walks of his. I'd started to wonder whether maybe on one of those walks, he'd maybe wandered near a cave, where he'd maybe made some strange moaning noises and –

My mom had just shot that idea down in flames.

Oh well, it wasn't a great idea anyway. I shivered as I remembered the moan. It was eerie. Creepy. Not like a human voice.

Jesse nudged me and pointed at the other end of the porch. Natalie was flopped on a lawn chair like a sack of flour. Eyes closed. Mouth open. A little trickle of drool ran down her chin.

I glanced at my watch. 10:36 A.M. Who takes a nap in the middle of the morning?

As we stood there staring, Hugo came running up the porch stairs. He hurled his scarf at Jesse and jumped into his arms. Jesse laughed, swung the little boy into the air, and gently put him down. Giggling, Hugo picked up his scarf and threw it at me. I caught it, grabbed Hugo as he leaped at me, and swung him around the way Jesse had. Hugo shrieked with happiness. When I put him down, he picked up the scarf again. This time, he threw it toward Natalie.

"HUGO! NO!" yelled Jesse.

But the little guy was already moving, charging across the porch like a bullet. He was aimed straight at – Natalie's stomach!

Lucky for Natalie, Jesse's on the relay team. He flew across the porch and caught Hugo while the kid was still in the air – a millisecond away from disaster.

WHUMP! Jesse landed, Hugo on top of him, on the floor.

I glanced at Natalie. Not even a flicker. Jesse made a funny noise – sort of a croak – and passed Hugo to me. I took him down the steps and set him on the grass.

"You'd better be nice to Jesse," I told him. "He just saved your life."

Hugo tossed his scarf in the air. "Hugo JUG-GING!" he yelled.

"Yeah, well. Don't be jugging around Natalie anymore, you hear?"

Aunty Edna backed out of the house a moment later, carrying a tray full of lemonade and fresh-baked apple muffins. We all gathered around. The muffins could have done with more sugar, and they were about twice as heavy as your average supermarket muffin. Still, they were better than most of the food around the aunts' house. I ate two.

Afterward, the twins begged Uncle Archie for a "show," and he gave us an acrobatics demonstration.

Handstands. Headstands. Cartwheels. He could walk on his hands and do flips too, back and front. It was like the guy was made out of rubber.

"What did you actually do in the circus, Uncle Archie?" asked my mom. "I mean, what was your act?"

"A little bit of a lot of things," said Uncle Archie. "Over the years, I did some clowning, some high wire, some animal work –"

"Animals?" Kevin's – or maybe Kenneth's – eyes lit up. "Lion taming?"

Uncle Archie laughed. "No. Much smaller animals, I'm afraid. Dogs mostly."

"Oh." Kevin looked disappointed.

"Horses too," added Uncle Archie. "And sometimes elephants."

"Elephants?" Kevin perked up again.

"Sure," said Uncle Archie. "Got stepped on one time. Ever get stepped on by an elephant?"

The twins' heads moved back and forth in unison.

"It hurts," said Uncle Archie. "Especially if the elephant won't get off." He turned to Jesse. "Ever tried to move an elephant?"

Jesse shook his head.

Uncle Archie tapped his temple. "You've got to use psychology. You've got to outsmart him."

"I bet you're really smart, Uncle Archie," said Kenneth. Or maybe Kevin.

"Smart enough, my young friend." Staring off into space, he added quietly, "At least, I hope I am."

Jesse and I exchanged glances.

After lunch, it started to rain, and we all crowded

inside. Aunty Edna brought out a Bingo game and an ancient-looking box of chocolates.

"They're from Christmas," she said, plunking the chocolates on the table. "I thought we could use them as prizes."

Everyone stared. The clear plastic covering was torn and yellow and curled up at the edges. "Season's Greetings," said the old-fashioned lettering.

"Christmas of what year?" Jesse hissed in my ear.

"Just try not to win," I whispered back.

I was lucky. I won only two Bingo's. One maraschino cherry and one caramel toffee. They both looked sort of … gray.

By the end of the afternoon, Jesse had won five.

"I think I'll save this for later," he said loudly, tucking his second orange cream into his shorts pocket. "Don't want to spoil my dinner."

Aunty Ivy patted his hand. "Edna's making pizza. We've heard how much you kids like pizza."

The thought of pizza cheered me up … until I saw the steaming trays. Who ever heard of a vegetable pizza? It wasn't pizza at all! It was dough covered in a layer of the day's garden pickings. Peas, beans, corn.

Cucumbers!

The thin layer of cheddar cheese on top didn't help one bit.

Even the adults had trouble with it. My mom gave Aunt Edna her usual compliments, but I saw her picking off bits of soggy cucumber.

As we left the table, Natalie caught hold of my arm. "Can I talk to you?"

"Sure." I let her pull me outside, onto the porch. The air was damp from the rain, but the wicker furniture was dry. Natalie settled us onto a couple of chairs and looked around to make sure we were alone.

"Can I sleep in your tent tonight? With you and Aunt Valerie?"

"Huh? I thought you had a cot in Aunt Ivy's room."

"I do." Lifting a finger to her mouth, she chewed nervously on a purple-painted nail. "I can't take it, Stevie. She's driving me nuts."

"Aunt Ivy? What's wrong? Does she snore?"

"Snore? I *wish*. She has weird nightmares. She moans and talks in her sleep." Natalie shivered and rubbed her arms.

"Nightmares?" I remembered what my mom had said about Aunty Ivy's nightmares. "What does she say?"

"Well, mostly she calls out in this scared voice – to Uncle Archie. It's like she's dreaming they're both in danger or something. She says things like 'dark' and 'falling.' Even 'dead.' It's creepy."

I grabbed her by the shoulders. "Natalie, this is important. Can you remember anything else?"

She nodded. "Did you ever hear of a place called Arlenville? Because she keeps mentioning that too. Over and over, all night long. Arlenville! Arlenville!"

"Arlenville?" Now she had me puzzled. Where was Arlenville?

Then it hit me. Not Arlenville.

Orville!

"Was it Orville, Natalie? Was that what she was saying?"

She thought for a moment. "Maybe. Sure, I think you're right. Orville! How did you know, Stevie?"

"Lucky guess. Did she say anything else?"

"Not really. Just lots of moaning. I stuck a pillow over my head."

I chewed on my lip, trying to think. Aunt Ivy? Talking in her sleep? Moaning about Orville Frisk? What did it mean? The word that really worried me was "dead."

Natalie's voice interrupted my thoughts. "So what do you say? Is it okay if I sleep in your tent?"

"It's only a two-person tent," I told her, "and we're already —"

Wait a minute. This could be a great opportunity.

I didn't *want* to spend the night in Aunty Ivy's room. I'd heard plenty of moaning already that day, thank you very much. But maybe, with a little encouragement, Aunt Ivy might let out a few secrets in her sleep. Secrets she wouldn't tell in the daytime.

"Listen, Natalie, why don't we trade places? You sleep in the tent, and I'll sleep in Aunt Ivy's room."

Her eyes widened. "Really, Stevie? Fabulous! I'll get my stuff." Before I could change my mind, she was gone.

I didn't get much chance to talk to Jesse before bedtime. That's the problem with family reunions — there's always somebody from your *family* hanging around. But I caught him after his shower and brought him up to date.

He was horrified. "You're going to lie there in the dark ... and listen to her moan?"

When he put it that way, it didn't sound so hot. "I'll get valuable information."

He grunted. "You're braver than I am, Stevie Diamond."

I wasn't, actually. But Natalie was already inside my tent, snuggled in my sleeping bag. Besides, it was just Aunty Ivy, right? Sure, she'd be having horrible nightmares. Sure, she'd be moaning in the dark about a dead guy. But it was still just Aunty Ivy.

I reminded myself of this fact half an hour later, at lights-out time.

"Sweet dreams, Stevie dear."

Aunt Ivy *looked* like the most harmless person you ever saw, in her purple dotted nightgown and her white face cream, fluffing up her pillow. But if there's one thing I've learned as a detective, it's this: don't believe everything you see.

In fact, don't believe *anything* you see.

I lay back on the cot. Aunty Ivy turned out the light.

Now all I had to do was wait.

Let the moaning begin.

CHAPTER

I DON'T *THINK* AUNT IVY HAD ANY NIGHTMARES THAT night. But I can't say for sure, seeing as how I fell asleep before you could say "Orville Frisk."

I slept like a rock too, waking up only once – just before dawn. The room was hushed and hazy, barely light enough to see the outlines of Aunty Ivy's white dresser and desk. I propped myself up on one elbow and squinted. Aunty Ivy was sleeping as peacefully as an actor in a mattress commercial.

Sounds were coming from somewhere though. Steps. Someone was walking. Going to the bathroom? Nope, it seemed to be coming from the next room. Aunt Edna's room. A pattern kept repeating. Six steps, a pause. Six steps, a pause.

Pacing – that's what it was. Aunt Edna was pacing on the other side of the wall. Back and forth she walked, back and forth. People pace when they're nervous, right? When they have something awful on their mind and can't sleep?

One more bit of evidence – as if I needed it – that things weren't right at the aunts' house. Fainting. Nightmares. Pacing. I'd never been to a family reunion before, but I was sure *this* stuff wasn't normal. Closing my eyes, I tried to make sense of it all.

When I opened them again, sunlight filled the room. Aunt Ivy was at her dresser, combing her hair.

"Morning, roommate. Did you sleep well? You certainly seemed to."

"What do you mean?

She smiled. "All that snoring."

Snoring? Me?

"Not that I minded," she added. "It was very … friendly."

Snoring. Ha!

Downstairs in the kitchen, there was good news. Aunt Patricia had managed to take over the kitchen long enough to make pancakes. Breakfast was heaven!

"Hmmph!" said Aunt Edna, poking at a pancake. "Not much nutrition in *that*."

Nutrition or not, she ate four. I forced myself to stop at six.

Afterward, I did my best to sneak off with Jesse before we got dragged into some family event. A reunion, I was beginning to realize, was like quicksand. It could suck you in and drag you down. Meals, chores, games, group activities … you could get buried alive in this family stuff.

We were halfway through the door when we got nabbed.

"Stevie?" said my mom. "Kenneth and Kevin are

hoping to go down to Old Point Beach today. They're a little young to go on their own. Could you and Jesse –"

"Aw, Mom. Geez. Can't Natalie –"

"Natalie's still sleeping."

Sure. In my tent!

"I'll bring the cards," said a twin. Kenneth, maybe. He held up a deck.

"I'll get our bathing suits," said the other twin.

"Sheesh!" muttered Jesse.

Old Point Beach is the only sandy beach on Catriola Island. The others are all rocky or covered in tiny round pebbles. Old Point has another advantage – a long boulder-covered spit of land that goes out into the water and curls around, creating a shallow bay. The water in the little bay comes and goes with the tide. Today the tide was in, and the bay was filled with gently lapping water. A couple of moms sat on the sand with toddlers who were digging holes and building castles. In the water, an old man swam slowly on his back. I shook off my annoyance.

"Last one in is a rotten –" I spotted the cards in Kenneth's hand. "– fish!"

The twins had identical bathing suits, of course. Gray, with red stripes down the sides. Just before we went in the water, I stole a peek at their feet. First time I'd seen them without socks. They were big – definitely Cooper feet – and a little pudgy, but otherwise normal. No extra toes or anything. I counted.

The beach turned out to be a good idea – even if it did come from my mom. After all the cave exploring, it felt great to paddle around in sunshine. The moms and little kids packed up after a while, and there was nobody left at the beach except us and the old man, who fell asleep in the shade of a tree. Jesse and I lay back on our towels, drying off. The twins perched on a log beside us.

"Want to play – hey, what's that?" said a twin. He pointed to a spot out in the bay.

Shielding my eyes, I searched the water. There! A dark nose poking above the surface. Long whiskers. Shiny black eyes.

"A seal!" I said.

Jesse sat up.

The seal's head bobbed around as it peered in different directions. Did it see us? If so, it didn't seem worried. It swam along the surface for a bit, then with a little flip, dove under.

"Can we go swim with it?" asked a twin.

I shook my head. "It'll swim away."

It didn't mind us looking, though. We watched quietly as the seal swam, bobbed under, surfaced again. It could stay underwater for a long time – way longer than us. Finally, after a really long dive, it disappeared. We spotted it out past the spit, its head getting smaller.

"Cool," said Jesse, his mouth still half open in a smile.

I nodded. "Sometimes a pod of killer whales comes past the island. My dad and I saw them once."

The memory was as clear as a photograph – twelve huge black backs, flippers upright, rising above the surface and then diving, rising and diving. One of them breached while we watched – leaping above the water, so we could see its enormous white underbelly and wide tail. It landed with a mighty splash.

The seal didn't come back. But later, as we searched for shells in the area close to the spit, I saw a flash of fur among the rocks. I whispered to the others to keep quiet. A moment later, a sea otter wiggled around a boulder. Its body was long and skinny, the dark fur slick and shiny. It shimmied over the boulder on tiny legs before vanishing behind a log. We waited for a long time, but it didn't peek out again.

When it was time to head back, I suggested that we walk along the beach instead of the road. It would take longer, but I had an idea. Maybe Jesse and I could still do some detecting – even with the twins in tow.

All along the beach, back from the water, houses squatted among the trees. Most were small weathered cottages built a long time ago. Here and there, people sat outside, relaxing on decks or in lawn chairs. A few swimmers splashed in the water. A group of kayakers paddling close to shore waved to us.

I checked out each house as we passed. One of them was Hank's, but I wasn't sure which. A twin helped me out.

"Hey, look! There's Hank."

He was sitting at a picnic table in front of a ramshackle green cottage with stacks of wood piled up the sides. He was staring straight down at the table, as if he was reading or eating. But there was no food or book in front of him. He was just staring. When the twins called out, he turned our way.

Hank looked awful. There were dark hollows around his eyes, and his face was all saggy, like a balloon losing air. He needed a shave too.

The twins didn't notice – they're not exactly what you'd call sensitive. But Jesse's eyes narrowed as we stopped beside the table.

"Oh ... hi, kids. What are you doing here?" Hank straightened up to face us.

I let the twins give him a report on the seal and the otter. He told us a couple of stories about animals he'd run into on the island – deer, snakes, raccoons. But you could tell his heart wasn't in it. The last story just kind of petered out.

"Never mind. You don't want to hear about that," he finished gloomily. "You kids want something to eat?"

Hank's snack was as halfhearted as his stories – a box of salted crackers and some apples that had been sitting around about a week too long. The twins sat down on either side of him and dived right in. I wasn't surprised. They stuffed their faces on Aunt Edna's cooking too. They could probably eat anything.

Me? I had something more important than food on my mind. Hank was part of the Orville Frisk story. He had been there forty-five years ago, when Archie left. He could probably tell us everything – *if* we could get him to talk.

I decided to ease into it. Make him feel relaxed.

"Must be great to see Uncle Archie after all these years," I said.

"Mmmnn," said Hank, studying the table as if it were a test he had to pass.

"Your oldest buddy," I continued hopefully.

"Mmmnn." He picked up a withered apple and ripped off a third of it in a single bite.

Kenneth opened a cracker-filled mouth. "Uncle Archie taught me and Kevin to juggle."

"That's right," I said enthusiastically. "Uncle Archie's a really helpful, friendly guy." I turned back to Hank. "He must have been fun to hang around with. Back in the old days, I mean."

Hank mumbled an answer. But he was talking to his chest now – and had his mouth full of apple besides – so all I caught was "Archie Cooper."

Jesse, who'd been listening quietly all this time, decided to do a little detective work of his own. But he made the same mistake I had made with Mr. Priddy. He went too far too fast.

"Uncle Archie's been really friendly to me," he said, "and I'm a *stranger* on the island. Was he always this friendly to … *strangers?* You know, back when he was young?"

Hank's head jerked up. His eyes narrowed, and he gave Jesse a long, searching look. "I'd best get back to work," he muttered. Leaving the apple cores and cracker box on the table, he disappeared into the house.

And that, of course, was that.

"What?" said Jesse, holding out his hands. "What did I do?"

As we headed back to the beach, I tried to encourage the twins to walk ahead, so Jesse and I could talk. But they stuck like glue, whispering and giggling. I tried to ignore them.

It was a good thing I couldn't. Out of the stream of babble, I picked out Hank's name. I grabbed Kevin's arm. "Kevin? What did you say? About Hank?"

He glanced back, surprised. "I'm Kenneth, Stevie. I was talking about what Hank said back at the table – about how he's a princess."

I yanked him to a stop. "Tell me – exactly – what Hank said."

The four of us formed a little circle on the beach. Kenneth smiled at each of us in turn, looking important.

"It was when you talked about him and Uncle Archie being friends. Hank said a funny thing."

"What?"

"He said 'If that's Archie Cooper, I'm Princess Anne.'"

Both twins covered their mouths and giggled.

It took a few seconds for the words to penetrate my brain. It took a few seconds longer for me to understand what they meant. My head slowly turned. My eyes met Jesse's.

"Don't you think that's funny?" asked Kenneth, snickering behind a hand. "Hank's a princess!"

"Yeah, funny." I turned him around so he was facing the right direction and gave him a little push. The twins shuffled off down the beach, shoulders hunched, laughing.

"Did you hear *that?*" Jesse whispered as soon as they were out of range. "Hank thinks Archie's not really Archie. He thinks the guy's a fake!"

Feeling a little dizzy, I put a hand on Jesse's shoulder for balance. Was it possible? Sure it was. The second I heard it, I knew it was possible. More than possible.

"How could it be?" asked Jesse. "The guy's staying with Edna and Ivy, for crying out loud. Archie's sisters! If he's *not* Archie, wouldn't they know?"

I shook my head. "Maybe not. Think about how long Archie's been gone. And think about what the aunts are like. Aunt Edna can hardly see her own feet without her glasses. Aunt Ivy's blind too, but in a different way. She only sees what's good in people."

"So … you figure it's true?" said Jesse.

"Shhh, let me think." My brain felt like it had Ping-Pong balls bouncing around in it. What did we know about this Uncle Archie, anyway? Did he *look* like Archie? Who knew? The only photos I had ever seen of Archie were blurry grayish ones from when he was a little kid.

Okay. So did he look like the Cooper family? He was bald. Hard to say if he'd had the curly Cooper hair. Suddenly, I remembered his small, trim feet – the only Cooper feet I'd ever seen that weren't huge.

Jesse was frowning with concentration. "Hey, Stevie? Remember what you told me about the night you arrived? You said Uncle Archie told stories about his Catriola childhood."

I thought back. "That's right! He did. But you know what? He told them like a list – like he was trying to convince us. His stories didn't sound real, Jessie! Not like things that had actually happened to him."

"Still, he did know some stories, right? So where did he learn them?"

"I don't know."

"And he can do circus tricks," Jesse pointed out. "Where did he learn those?"

"I don't know, I don't know. It's too confusing." Ping-Pong balls flew everywhere in my brain!

I paused. Shut my eyes. Took a deep breath. Then another. Focus, Stevie, focus. Deep down inside, I was starting to get a feeling – in my bones. I waited. It got stronger … and stronger. It happens sometimes. It's happened on other cases. My bones don't lie.

I opened my eyes. "Hank's right. The guy's an imposter."

"Imposter?"

"A fake."

"But … but," said Jesse, fumbling for words, "if he's not Uncle Archie, then who *is* he?"

The same thought hit both of us at the same time. We said it together. "Orville Frisk?"

The thought died immediately. "Couldn't be," I said. "Mr. Priddy said Frisk was tall, remember? A beanpole. This guy's on the short side. He's not Frisk."

"Then who *is* he?" Jesse repeated. "What's he doing here?"

I shook my head. "I don't know. But it's scary.

This total stranger staying with the aunts? He could be anyone!"

Jesse's eyes darted back and forth nervously. "He could be – Jack the Ripper!"

"Jack the Ripper's dead, Jesse."

"He is?"

I nodded. "But it's a good point. This guy could be dangerous."

"I'm not afraid of a little, er, danger," said Jesse. "Listen, Stevie, we'd better do something. Soon!"

"Right," I agreed. "What?"

"I don't know. Don't you have any ideas?"

I sighed. Then I shook my head.

Not one.

For an experienced detective, I was feeling pretty darned clueless.

CHAPTER

JESSE AND I STOPPED TALKING WHEN WE CAUGHT UP with the twins, but they must have sensed that something was up. The rest of the way home, they stuck closer than gum to a shoe. Kenneth (I think it was Kenneth) actually rubbed elbows with me as we walked down the beach. It was kind of weird because he didn't say anything – just sidled along really close, staring up into my ear.

"Can you give me a little room here? I'm trying to think."

I concentrated as hard as I could, trying to figure things out. Mostly, I was looking for the answer to a really important question. How did this fake-Archie thing fit in with all the other weird stuff that had been happening? There had to be some connection. The Ping-Pong balls started bouncing around in my head again – Orville Frisk, the gold, the cave, Aunt Ivy's nightmares. Oy! Everything got more and more mixed up.

Suddenly, I knew what I had to do.

Write it all down! Make notes. It works every time for me. If I put my ideas in black and white on paper, I can *see* what I'm thinking.

The problem was – Kenneth. I couldn't get rid of him. Not then. Not back at the house, where he almost sat in my lap as we ate some leftover sandwiches from lunch. Not even after lunch, when the other boys – Kevin and Jesse – started helping Hugo to build a space station out of blocks. Kenneth was right beside me when I asked Aunty Ivy for a notepad. He was right beside me when I found a pen in the kitchen drawer. And he was *still* right beside me when I sat down on the back porch to make notes.

"Um, Kenneth? I'd like to be alone."

"It's Kevin." He stared fondly at my teeth.

"Sure, fine. Did you hear the part about … alone?"

He looked around the empty porch. "We *are* alone, Stevie."

I did the only thing a girl can do at a time like that.

"Be right back," I said – and ducked into the bathroom. A firm click of the lock, and I was finally by myself. Perching on the only seat available, I pulled out my pen and paper.

What we had here, I realized, was three different mysteries. Quickly, I wrote them down:

MYSTERIES

1. WHERE IS THE LOST KLONDIKE GOLD?
2. WHAT HAPPENED TO ORVILLE FRISK?
3. WHO IS THE ARCHIE IMPOSTER?

The first two mysteries were connected. Mr. Priddy had made that clear. And the third? Well, I was pretty sure that one was connected too. I had no proof, but I could *feel* it. In my bones.

So the question was – *how* was the fake Uncle Archie connected to Orville Frisk and the lost Klondike gold?

I thought back over all the conversations I'd had with Archie. Had he ever said anything about lost Klondike gold? Never. Had he ever said anything about Orville Frisk? No. In fact, he was the only one of the old people who *hadn't* gone all weird about Frisk's hat.

A twin-ish voice came through the door. "Hey, Stevie? Are you in there?"

"No!"

Giggle giggle. "Yes, you are."

"Go away, Kevin."

"It's Kenneth."

"Go away anyhow."

Closing my eyes, I tried to concentrate. What about suspicious behavior? Had Uncle Archie ever said or done anything suspicious? Definitely a yes. Those walks to get "fresh air"? Ha!

Then, like a whack across the head, it hit me.

The night Jesse and I had slept in the living room – skunk night – we had caught Uncle Archie red-handed, wandering around with a flashlight. I'd wondered at the time why he needed a flashlight, why he hadn't just turned on the light. He didn't even know Jesse and I were there, so he couldn't have been worried about waking us up.

A voice came through the door again. "Stevie?"

"GO AWAY!"

"It's Aunt Cheryl, Stevie. There's a lineup out here. Are you going to be long?"

Uh-oh.

"Be right out!" I yelled.

Scribbling fast, I started a new section on the paper:

SUSPICIOUS BEHAVIOR

UNCLE ARCHIE - "FRESH AIR" DISAPPEARANCES
          - SKULKS AT NIGHT WITH A FLASHLIGHT

I had barely gotten it down when I remembered what else had happened on skunk night. Jesse had found the *Tom Sawyer* book – along with the map to the cave.

It hit me like a second whack across the head – suddenly I understood why Archie was in the living room that night. He hadn't come downstairs for warm milk! He hadn't even gone into the kitchen. He'd been skulking around the bookcase. He was looking for a book. A book with a map! A map that would lead him to Bat Cave! He was looking for *Tom Sawyer*!

But he hadn't found it. Jesse had! And that meant – probably – that Archie hadn't found Bat Cave either. Whack again – I remembered those mysterious disappearances. He wasn't looking for fresh air. He was looking for Bat Cave!

It was all coming clear.

The fake Uncle Archie was after the lost Klondike gold.

But … who *was* he?

A voice came through the door. "Stephanie? Are you in there? It's your Aunty Edna."

I jumped to my feet.

"Now you listen here, young lady, there's such a thing as common courtesy. Unless you're sick, I don't see that you have any excuse at *all* for monopolizing the bathroom."

When I opened the door, Kenneth, Aunty Cheryl and Aunty Edna were standing there in a line, waiting. I coughed a little, patted my chest and tried to look feverish. Aunty Edna's jaw, which was already sticking out like a bulldog's, edged out farther.

I ducked past quickly and headed for the living room.

Jesse, Hugo and Kevin were just finishing the space station, so I plopped into a nearby armchair to wait. With the twins busy, I had a chance to read over my list. It looked good. I especially liked the "Suspicious Behavior" section. Only it wasn't complete. A *lot* of people had been acting suspiciously around here. Better add the rest of them. I started scribbling.

"Stevie?"

My mom was standing in the doorway, arms crossed. "Have you been teasing Kenneth? Aunty Edna says you wouldn't let him use the bathroom."

"No. I mean, yes. I mean –"

"Honestly, Stevie." She let out a big sigh and pushed her hair off her forehead. "I thought you were past that sort of thing."

"You don't understand, Mom. I –"

"Never mind. We'll be off in the morning, and Kenneth can have the bathroom to himself."

"He can – what?"

"We're taking the eleven o'clock ferry back to Vancouver tomorrow. I phoned your dad to meet us."

"But, Mom! You can't. We – NO!"

She gave me a puzzled frown. "I thought you'd be pleased." Coming a few steps closer, she dropped her voice to a whisper. "After all your complaints about coming here."

"I know, but it's ... it's different now."

"What about the food?" she asked, still whispering.

"It's ... not so bad." If I'd been Pinocchio, my nose would have grown right through the front window.

My mind raced. How could I get her to stay? There was no way I could just *tell* her Uncle Archie was an imposter. My mom's the kind of person who needs solid proof to believe anything. Jesse and I had nothing but the word of a nine-year-old and ... my bones.

But how could we leave the aunties? The other relatives would be going home soon too. The aunties would be all alone, out in the country, abandoned and helpless, with – Archie the Ripper!

A movement from the space station on the floor caught my eye. Jesse was making faces behind his hand. The message was clear. Convince her to stay.

"We can't leave, Mom. We're ... having too much fun!"

Weak, Stevie. Really weak. I knew it as soon as the words were out of my mouth. *Fun* is not a convincing reason for any mom, especially mine. Desperate, I carried on.

"We've been hiking ... and exploring ... and swimming ..."

"And getting tons of exercise," added Jesse from the floor.

Exercise! Good one! Moms like exercise.

"We've seen lots of nature too," Jesse added. "Seals, otters, woodpeckers. It'll probably really help us in science next year."

Wow! The boy was hot. If anything could convince her to stay, it was the chance of an educational experience.

My mom smiled. "I'm glad you've learned so much, Jesse. And I'm sure Edna and Ivy will be glad to have you visit again. But this reunion's tiring for them. I think we should go home and give them a chance to get to know Archie better. On their own."

"On their *own?* But, Mom –"

She held up a hand. "Enough, Stevie."

The space station project ended with a crash a moment later, when Hugo jumped on it. Jesse grabbed my arm. We ran out to the garden and scrunched down behind a row of tall sunflowers.

"We *can't* leave!" he said.

"I know. I've figured out why the fake Archie's here. He's after the lost Klondike gold." Quickly I explained what I'd figured out about Archie's late-night skulking with his flashlight.

Jesse nodded. "You're right! He was looking for the book. It fits."

I showed him my notes. With the additions I'd made in the living room, they looked like this:

MYSTERIES

1. WHERE IS THE LOST KLONDIKE GOLD?
2. WHAT HAPPENED TO ORVILLE FRISK?
3. WHO IS THE ARCHIE IMPOSTER?

SUSPICIOUS BEHAVIOR

UNCLE ARCHIE	- "FRESH AIR" DISAPPEARANCES
	- SKULKS AT NIGHT WITH A FLASHLIGHT
AUNT IVY	- UPSET ABOUT HAT
	- MOANS "ORVILLE" IN NIGHTMARES
AUNT EDNA	- UPSET ABOUT HAT
	- PACES IN THE NIGHT
HANK	- UPSET ABOUT HAT
	- LOOKS WORRIED AND ANXIOUS
	- SAYS ARCHIE ISN'T ARCHIE

Jesse read quickly, brushing away a wasp that was hovering around his head.

"Good work, Stevie. But what are we going to do about your mom? She'll make us leave. You have to stop her."

I shook my head. "Might as well try to stop a freight train."

"What if we just tell the aunts what we know? What we heard from Hank – about Uncle Archie being an imposter."

I shook my head again. "Wouldn't work. *We* didn't hear anything. The twins heard it. Only one twin, actually."

Jesse winced. "Okay, but here's what I don't understand. If Hank knows Archie's a fake, why hasn't *he* told the aunts?"

"Excellent question. I'd ask him, but I know what he'd say. 'Mmmnn.'"

Jesse reached into the tomato patch and yanked out a stray weed we had missed. "I have a feeling Hank's hiding a few secrets of his own," he said.

"You can say that again. This case has more secrets than a surprise party. Nobody – I mean nobody – is telling us the whole story."

"So what are we going to do?"

Good question. What *could* we do to convince the family that "Uncle Archie" was a fake? How could we make them believe that this cheerful juggling grandpa was really a treasure-hunting imposter, here for the same reason as Orville Frisk – to look for the Klondike gold?

"We need proof." I drew a big "P" in the dirt. "Something solid. Something real. Something nobody can argue with."

Jesse snorted. "Oh sure, and we have –" He looked at his watch. "– nineteen hours to come up with it. How about a signed confession, Stevie? Or maybe a nice police photograph – Uncle Archie in Bat Cave holding a big sack of gold?"

I laughed. Then a thought hit me that cut off the laugh so quickly I almost choked.

"Hold it!" I said. "Stop. Go back. What did you just say?"

"You mean about the signed confession?"

"No – no."

"The photo? Uncle Archie in the cave?"

"Yes!" I grinned. "YES! You did it, Jesse! You figured out what we should do."

"I did?" He glanced around, as if I was confusing him with someone else. "But, Stevie, I was just kidding. I –"

"I know you were kidding. But don't you see? *We can actually do it!* We can get a picture of Uncle Archie coming out of Bat Cave. Maybe he won't be carrying a sack of gold, but just showing him there – at the cave – that's our proof! How could he deny that he's after the gold? How could he keep talking about 'fresh air'?"

Jesse held up both hands. "Wait a minute. You said he doesn't even know where the cave is."

"He doesn't," I said. "Not yet. He won't know until we give him *Tom Sawyer!*"

Jesse blinked. "We're going to give him the map?"

"Yes!" As quickly as the plan formed in my mind, I blurted it out to Jesse. "We'll leave the book lying around where he'll be sure to find it. When he does, he'll head straight for the cave. And *we'll* be right behind him. We'll take my mom's camera, and we'll snap a picture of him going in – and coming out. We'll use the telephoto lens, so we can take the picture from a distance. He won't even know we're there. There's one of those one-hour development machines in Priddy's Store, so we can have the pictures back tomorrow morning. Jesse, you're a genius!"

"I am?" He grinned. "Yeah, I guess I am."

I looked at my watch. "It's already four o'clock. We've got to move fast."

The problem with plans is – they don't always go as planned. I *did* manage to borrow my mom's camera. Then Jesse doctored the map to make it simpler to find the cave. He finished the "arb" so it read "arbutus tree" and added the words "look for crevice" after the part about "16 steps." That stuff was easy.

The hard part was getting Uncle Archie to find *Tom Sawyer*. No matter where we put it, he kept walking right past. We left it on the porch steps, on the coffee table and on the couch. He never gave it a glance. Aunt Cheryl spotted it on the couch and put it away in the bookcase.

Finally, Jesse noticed Archie's reading glasses on the dining room table. We laid the book, cover up, title obvious, right beside them.

Bingo! As Jesse and I played a fake game of cards at the far end of the table, Archie picked up his glasses, put them on and spotted the book. I heard him suck in his breath. He opened it immediately. And to the last page!

"Your move!" I told Jesse, whose mouth was hanging open just a little too wide, if Archie happened to look over.

No need to worry. Archie was way too engrossed in the map. When he finally did look up, all he saw was a couple of card-playing kids concentrating hard on their game. Snapping the book closed, he headed for the kitchen – and the back door. I grabbed my backpack with my mom's camera inside, and we got ready to follow.

That's when the next thing went wrong. Family reunion quicksand again. Aunt Edna's voice came from the kitchen. "Don't go running off now, Archie. Dinner's almost ready."

Seconds later, Archie was back. Strolling past us, he sat down, still holding the book, on the living room couch.

"What's he doing?" Jesse whispered.

"He's reading it," I said.

"Reading it? He's not supposed to be *reading* it. He's —"

"Shhhh!"

Archie didn't budge again till dinnertime. Then he kept the book on his lap the whole time we ate. Afterward, he went right back to the couch … and kept reading. We waited half an hour. An hour. An hour and forty minutes. Still reading. My mom curled up at the other end of the couch and started writing in her journal. Aunt Patricia read Hugo a bunch of picture books in the rocking chair. The minutes ticked by.

Jesse and I held a whispered conference on the shadowy landing of the stairs. We could watch Archie from there without being noticed.

"Rats!" I said. "It's not working. He's not going to the cave."

"Maybe he's waiting till tomorrow," said Jesse.

"He *can't* wait till tomorrow! We won't be here."

Jesse nodded, looking worried. "Well, how about if we … spook him?"

"Spook him?"

"Yeah." Jesse's voice was eager. "We could get him nervous. Make him think *we're* going to the cave in the morning. Make him think he has to make his move now."

"Spook him," I said slowly. "It might just work."

It worked like a charm. All I had to do was ask my mom if Jesse and I could go for one last hike – at dawn the next day. I told her we'd found an interesting place up on the ridge, and we wanted to go back and explore. She played right into our hands. It was amazing.

"Looking for the Klondike gold?" she said with a smile.

Perfect. Archie's head whipped around to face us. He almost dropped the book.

"Something like that," I said mysteriously. Jesse and I didn't speak again till we were safely back on the landing.

"That was great!" he whispered, pounding my shoulder with excitement.

"Ow!" I said. "Yeah, great. Take it easy."

We settled in to wait.

An hour later, Archie still hadn't made his move. Things had definitely changed though. He was restless – fidgeting and squirming as if he couldn't find a comfortable spot on the couch. The book was still open in front of him, but he had stopped turning the pages.

"What's he *doing?*" whispered Jesse, chewing on his thumbnail. "It'll be dark soon, Stevie. Why isn't he going to the cave?"

"Maybe he's planning to go later. You know … after everyone's gone to bed."

Jesse groaned.

"It's a good thing my mom's camera has a flash," I added.

Jesse looked at me as though I had two heads. "Excuse me? A flash? Do you seriously think I'm going back to that cave in the dark? It's scary enough in the daytime!"

I thought about the cave. The inky dampness. The hollowness of our footsteps. The beating of unseen wings. The stone walls closing in. Worst of all, the ghostly moaning.

"We *have* to go," I said, trying to convince myself as much as Jesse. "It's our last chance."

"Uh-uh. No way." He shook his head, really fast, really hard. "Remember those fluttering noises? We didn't *see* any bats, right? Want to know why? It's because vampires come out only at night! If we go after dark, all the garlic in the world isn't going to protect us."

"But what about the aunts?"

Jesse took a deep breath, then shook his head slowly. "I feel sorry about your aunts, Stevie. Really I do. But that cave at night … I can't handle it."

He shuddered. Shudders must be like yawns – catchy – because a big one ran through my body too.

I worked on him for the next ten minutes, but no luck. The thought of the cave was too scary. I tried a new approach.

"What if we took someone with us? There's safety in numbers, right? What if we took someone older?"

"Older? Who?"

"Well, not a lot older. I was thinking of ... Natalie."

"Natalie! Why would *she* come?"

Good question. I hadn't exactly figured that out yet. But she was our only choice. The twins were too young, and the others were all adults who wouldn't go along with our plan.

"She'll come," I said. "How about you?"

Jesse rubbed his chin. "Wellllllllll ... if there are three of us ... and if we stay *outside* the cave ... then I guess it wouldn't be *too* bad. I guess I could do that."

I grabbed his hand. "Let's go get her!"

We found Natalie lying on the cot in Aunty Ivy's room, slices of cucumber over her eyes. Her long reddish hair was spread out over the pillow like a fan. Thick cotton balls were stuck between her toes to keep the nail polish from smearing.

"What's with the cucumbers?" whispered Jesse.

I'd seen it in a magazine, so I explained. "It's supposed to be good for the skin around your eyes. So you don't get wrinkles."

"Wrinkles! She's fifteen!"

I shrugged.

"You go ahead," said Jesse. "Ask her. I'll stay outside the door here. If I peek over the bannister, I can keep an eye on you-know-who."

It would be too complicated to tell Natalie the whole story – even if she believed us, which she probably wouldn't. So I kept it simple. I told her we were curious about Uncle Archie's mysterious disappearances. I said we were planning to follow him if he went out later, and we wanted to have someone older with us.

"Sort of an adult, you know?" Maybe flattery would win her over.

"Not interested," she drawled. "It's been years since I played spy games. I have better things to do."

Like lie around with vegetables on your face? I didn't actually *say* it. Just thought it.

Jesse, listening from the doorway, stuck his head in. He pointed out that it would be an adventure and exciting, but I knew it wouldn't work. People like Natalie only understand one thing.

"I'll give you ten bucks," I said.

The cucumber slices shifted.

"Make it twenty."

"Fifteen. But you have to come with us, no matter how late it is."

Whipping off the cucumbers, Natalie sat up and held out her hand, palm up. "Deal!"

Personally, I thought it had gone really well. But as we settled down on the landing again, Jesse was all upset.

"I can't believe you paid her, Stevie. Nobody's ever paid *us* for detecting."

"It was the only way. We could try to convince her till morning and get nowhere."

Jesse shook his head. "It's not right. They're her aunts too. She should help for free."

"It's my money, Jesse."

"Still ..."

For the next hour, things were pretty quiet. I kept watch from the stairwell while Jesse poked around in the bookshelves. Finally, at ten o'clock, the relatives started heading for bed.

"I'll be there soon," I told Aunt Ivy. "Don't wait up for me."

Archie went upstairs a few minutes later, yawning conspicuously. Natalie headed outside to the tent. We'd invited her to keep watch with us, but she wasn't interested. I whispered that we'd come get her when it was time.

"Leave the zipper of the tent open," I told her, "so we don't wake my mom."

"Sure," said Natalie. "Whatever."

Jesse rolled his eyes. I could see he was wondering whether I'd get my fifteen bucks' worth. I was beginning to wonder, myself.

A hush settled over the house. The last lights went out. Jesse and I crept into a closet at the foot of the stairs. I was carrying the backpack. With a camera and two big flashlights inside, it was heavy. We left the closet door open a crack. Archie would have to walk past us to get outside.

We'd be waiting.

CHAPTER

IT TOOK LESS THAN AN HOUR.
The first thing we heard was the click of a door opening upstairs. I nudged Jesse, and we hunched motionless in the closet. Steps padded across the upstairs hall, then down the stairs. Suddenly the living room was lit up – dimly – by a flashlight's glow. We watched through the crack as the flashlight bobbed past. A moment later, we heard the *scrawk* of the back door opening, followed by a soft thud as it closed.

I counted to twenty. Jesse and I crept out of the closet, dashed to the back door and peered outside. Uncle Archie's flashlight was moving through the orchard in the direction of the path.

"Let's go!" I said. We raced toward the tents. The meadow was silver-bright under a full moon. Good. We wouldn't have to turn our flashlights on yet.

We stopped outside my mom's tent and listened.

"Your mom's asleep," whispered Jesse. "I can hear a snore."

"Make that two snores," I whispered back. "Natalie's asleep too."

We tiptoed to the tent door. I reached for the zipper, which was supposed to be open.

It wasn't. Darn that Natalie! The zipper was a big, rusty metal one that opened with a noise like an old fence being ripped apart.

Okay. Deal with it, Stevie. I thought about those safe-cracking burglars you see in the movies – the ones who have light, delicate fingers. Feeling around carefully, I found the thing you pull. With my light, delicate, safe-cracking fingers, I pulled.

PPRRRR-R-R-I-P-P-P!

"Shhh!!" hissed Jesse.

I tried again. Slower this time. Quieter. Carefully, I edged the zipper along, notch … by notch … by notch … by notch. Rats! This was going to take all night.

Jesse's voice was urgent. "Can you hurry it up? He's getting away."

It was, I realized, a choice – like that moment when you have to remove a bandage. Do you ease it off slowly, giving yourself a little pain that lasts a long time? Or do you take a deep breath and rip the sucker off in a single moment of agony?

I took a deep breath.

PPRRRR-R-R-I-P-P-P! From the bottom to the top of the tent door in one swift movement.

PPRRRR-R-R-I-P-P-P! From the bottom to the right corner in a second quick movement.

"Shh! Shh! Shh!" Jesse was going nuts behind me. He's the bandage-easing type. I held up a hand, and we waited. Listened.

144

Snores. Two different ones? Yes. Good.

Sneaking inside the tent, I crawled carefully over to where Natalie's head and shoulders should be. Grabbing one shoulder, I shook. Nothing. I shook harder. Her body rolled back and forth like a rag doll. I tried pinching a cheek. Blowing in an ear.

Nothing. She and my mom were snoring in harmony now – my mom a deep bass, Natalie a high, quavery treble.

There was only one thing to do. Crawling backward till I reached the door, I located a foot inside Natalie's sleeping bag. I grabbed hold and pulled. Backing through the door, I dragged Natalie – still inside her sleeping bag – out of the tent.

Jesse clutched his head with both hands. "What are you *doing?*"

"What does it *look* like I'm doing?" I hissed back. "Get over here and help me with Sleeping Beauty."

We hauled her a little ways away, and Jesse propped her up. Maybe it was the cool air, or maybe it was the serious shaking that Jesse and I gave her – she looked like she was in a blender – but something did the job.

"Whoossat? Whassat? Cut it –" bleated Natalie before I covered her mouth with my hand.

Fortunately, she had done one thing right. She was already dressed. Jesse and I each grabbed an arm and pulled her away from the tent so my mom wouldn't hear her complaining.

"For crying out – what the – stop – let go –"

I reminded her of the fifteen dollars that had moved from my pocket to hers earlier, and she calmed down. But I could still hear her muttering under her breath.

Jesse and I held a whispered conference. Uncle Archie had enough of a lead on us, we decided, that it was safe to use our flashlights. We headed for the orchard and then into the woods. Even with the lights on, it was tricky finding our way. Natalie was no help.

"Must have been out of my mind ... going to break an ankle ... freezing out here ... whose dumb idea ..."

The woods were cool and damp at night and so dark you'd have to be a raccoon to see. I looked up, searching for the moon, but all I could see was the high forest canopy, with a few little breaks where stars twinkled. We continued our slow climb, Jesse first, then Natalie, then me. I shone my flashlight ahead so that Natalie would know where to put her feet. You'd *think* she'd appreciate it.

"Where on earth ... can't see a thing ... fifteen lousy bucks ... trying to torture ..."

Finally, we reached the ridge. As we stepped out of the tall trees into the moonlight – brighter than it had been any night since we arrived – Jesse flicked off his flashlight. I did the same. We trudged up the last bit and stood at the top of the ridge. The view was incredible. There, across the water, was the city of Vancouver, lit up like a giant's birthday cake. Closer, out in the strait, a ferry boat passed, its rows of windows glowing. Closer still, on the slope below us, a lone light moved slowly and carefully through the darkness. I could see the dim outline of the man carrying it.

Archie!

We watched in silence – even Natalie was quiet for a few seconds – as the light shone up and down the arbutus tree. Yes, Archie, that's right. South now ... yes. Be careful. Yes. The light stopped at exactly the right spot. Then it circled around on the ground.

"What's he doing?" asked Natalie.

"Looking for the cave," Jesse whispered back.

"What cave? You didn't say anything about a cave."

"Keep your voice down," hissed Jesse.

The light stopped. It dropped lower. Then it disappeared, along with the dim figure carrying it.

"He found it!" said Jesse.

"What's going on here anyway?" whined Natalie.

"Come on," I said. "Let's get closer."

Natalie complained so much on the way down the slope that I began to feel *really* sorry we'd brought her along. Maybe we should give her a flashlight and send her back? Nope. If she got lost or hurt, it would be our fault. We were stuck with her. If only she would just – shut up!

"Ouch! ... eaten alive ... scratched to pieces ... of all the brainless, idiotic ..."

I made an important new rule for the rest of my life. Never *ever* take Natalie anywhere.

Jesse, who was in the lead and searching the ground ahead of him with his flashlight, held out his arm to stop us. We were there – just above the crevice. He sat down on some flattened bushes and pointed with his flashlight for us to sit beside him.

"How can I ... full of thorns ... can't see ... ow!"

"Natalie?"

"Yeah?"

"Two bucks bonus if you'll stop talking."

"Five," said Natalie.

"Three," I said.

"Deal."

"You're paying her *more?*" complained Jesse.

I didn't care. It was only money. Worth every penny too, as three dollars' worth of peace descended on the slope. We sat there in silence, staring into the crevice – a gaping black crack in the ground. We were right above the cave entrance.

"Got the camera?" whispered Jesse.

"I'll get it ready," I said.

"Camera?" said Natalie. "What's the –"

"Uh-uh-uh," I said. "A deal's a deal."

Silence followed, except for a few rustles and clicks as I got the camera out.

The plan Jesse and I had worked out, waiting in the closet, was this. The moment we saw – or heard – Archie coming out of the cave, we'd take a couple of quick flash photos. Archie would be semi-blinded by the flash, we figured, and he'd stumble around inside the crevice for a while. After that, it would take him a few minutes to find his way out in the dark and a few more minutes to climb up. By the time he got to the top of the slope, we'd be long gone down the path. We had the advantage of knowing the area in the daylight, so it should be easy to get back to the house without Archie ever knowing what hit him.

The one possible hitch, of course, was ... Natalie.

I decided not to think about that.

I don't know how much time passed with no sound except the hum of mosquitoes and an occasional slap. I do know that it was a long time – and getting longer. What could he be doing in there? I'd been in that cave twice, and I knew it didn't take this long to explore.

"What's he doing?" I asked Jesse finally.

"Beats me."

Did Archie know something we didn't? Did he know about some special place to hunt inside the cave? Something we'd missed? The thought made me nervous. What if he actually found the lost Klondike gold? Was that what was taking so long? Was he digging it up?

A jet flew high overhead, its lights flashing. Above us, the sky was crowded with stars. I decided to count to a hundred. He'd *have* to be out by then.

One, two ...

A hundred came and went. I did it again.

Okay, this was getting ridiculous. Where *was* he?

Suddenly, a horrible thought crossed my mind. What if there was a second way out of the cave? A route we'd missed. The fake Archie might have already made his escape. Sure! While the three of us sat here like monkeys, he'd be long gone, laughing all the way – a sack of Klondike gold clutched under his arm.

"I'm going in," I said.

A pause.

"What did you say?" whispered Jesse.

"I have to go in." Quickly, I explained why.

"But, Stevie, it could be dangerous. What if you – you don't come back? Your mom will blame me, and –"

"Then come with me."

"Come with you? But –"

"No buts, Jesse. I'm going. Now." I got to my feet and turned on my flashlight. You'd have to be a *real* idiot to try to climb down into the crevice without a light.

I could hear Jesse appealing to Natalie. "We have to go with her, Natalie. It's not safe to let her go alone."

"Baloney!" said Natalie. *"I'm* not going anywhere. Especially into some stupid cave!"

"But, Natalie –"

"Forget it."

I searched the crevice with my flashlight, looking for the easy way down. Jesse, meanwhile, was frantically trying to persuade Natalie. I could have told him he was wasting his breath.

"Okay," he said finally, his voice desperate, "I'll … I'll give you … five dollars if you'll come."

Was I hearing things?

"Make it ten," said Natalie.

"Okay, okay, okay. Ten dollars! That's all the money I have in the whole world, Natalie, except for my savings that I can't take out until college, and I hope you're satisfied!"

"Deal," said Natalie.

She got to her feet. So did Jesse.

"No crawling," she added. "If I have to crawl, it's five bucks extra."

I let out a sigh. How could I be *related* to this person?

We crept down into the crevice, me first, followed by Natalie, followed by Jesse. When we got to the cave entrance, we turned out the flashlights. We'd have to do this in total dark.

"Watch your hair," whispered Jesse.

"My hair?" said Natalie. "Why –"

"Uh-uh-uh," I said.

We stepped inside, into inky blackness. Stopped. Listened.

Nothing.

Archie must be in the second cavern.

It's a good thing I hadn't had much chance to really *think* about going back into the cave. Now that I was inside, the terror of our last visit came flooding back. My knees felt weak. I reached out and clutched at the cold, damp stone.

Take it easy, I told myself.

Holding on to the wall, I forced myself to take a step. Natalie's fingernails were buried in my upper arm as she followed. Slowly, with no sound but the shuffle of our feet, the three of us edged around the wall of the cave. I had to feel my way, trying to remember the shape of the cave, its size, its bumps and lumps and twists. How far had we gone? How close were we to the passage?

We were – I figured – maybe halfway around

when I heard a sound. But it was coming from *behind* us. A scraping. Then a thunk. A couple of footsteps ... then a couple more.

Coming closer!

I whirled around.

White light filled the cavern, blinding me.

CHAPTER

M Y KNEES, ALREADY MUSHY, BUCKLED. I ALMOST fell.

Jesse let out a frightened squawk. Then he clicked on his flashlight. Its beam wavered, then focused on a spot just above where the other light was coming from.

"Aunty Ivy!" gasped Natalie. "What are *you* doing here?"

Aunt Ivy's squinting face came clear in the flashlight beam, her hair wild and frizzy. She had just stepped through the entrance into the cave.

"Never mind me," said Aunt Ivy, dragging her flashlight beam across our faces. "What are *you* doing here? And you, Stevie. And Jesse. Are the twins here too?"

"No," I gulped, trying to figure out which of my hundred questions to ask first. Not that it mattered. Aunty Ivy was doing all the talking.

"Shame on you kids, running off like that. How do you think I felt, Stevie, when I woke up – out of a nightmare yet – and saw that you weren't there? Thank goodness I spotted your flashlights moving through the orchard. I knew right away what you kids were up to. I knew you were coming here. It's that hat! Ever since I saw that cursed hat, I've been afraid something like this would happen."

"Aunt Ivy," I said, "how did you —"

"This place is dangerous!" she interrupted in a harsh whisper. "You shouldn't be here. You have no idea what horrible things have —"

She stopped. Suddenly her hand appeared in front of her face, one finger raised to cover her lips. She glanced toward the cave entrance.

"Someone's coming," she whispered. "Turn off your light. Follow me."

We — four of us now — moved together, as quickly as we could across the cavern. For a moment, there was no sound but the shuffling of our feet. Then we stopped. Listened.

From the cave entrance came a new sound.

A soft moan.

Oh no.

Another moan …

A dim light.

Aunty Ivy's voice was thin and quivery as she whispered, "It's … him!"

Orville's ghost! It *had* to be.

I tried to think. No time! Out of the blackness, Natalie's hand reached out and gripped mine.

"Stevie! Jesse!" she hissed in a fierce whisper. "Let's *get* him!"

The next thing I knew, I was hurtling across the cavern. Natalie was pulling me, pulling us both,

Jesse and me. Toward the moan. Toward the dim light. We were – what? Attacking? Yes, attacking! But attacking who? Attacking what?

"GYAAAAAHH!" yelled Jesse in the old war cry I recognized from our first case.

When I heard that cry – as scared as I was, as confused as I was – I couldn't stop myself.

"GYAAAAAHH!" I screamed.

Natalie joined in too. "GYAAAAAHH!"

The three of us dived onto whatever it was, wrestling it to the ground. I don't know what I expected, but whatever we'd tackled was big and chunky and sort of squishy. The moaning was horrible.

Aunt Ivy had clicked her flashlight on again, and she rushed over to where the three of us were sitting on –

Aunty Edna!

"Oh, for Pete's sake!" said Aunty Ivy. "You kids – get up! Get off her."

We were on our feet the second we saw Aunt Edna's scowling face. She was still moaning as we helped her up.

"Are you all right?" asked Ivy.

"All right? How can I be all right? I've been assaulted by a gang of hooligans!" Aunty Edna let out a moan of outrage. Hearing it up close, I realized that it was nothing like the ghostly moans from our last visit.

"For goodness sake, Edna, what are you *doing* here?" Ivy sounded annoyed herself. "It's the middle of the night. How do you even know about this cave?"

When Edna heard that, she got furious. "How do *I* know about it! How do *you* know about it? How dare you speak to me that way, Ivy! And you brought your thugs with you too, I see. I suppose you're responsible for the behavior of these — these punks!"

Thugs? Punks? Us?

The aunties continued to hiss insults at each other. Since they were both talking at the same time, it was hard to make out what they were saying. The only clear thing was that they were both spitting mad.

In the middle of it all, Jesse suddenly said, "Shhhh!"

They stopped — we all stopped — and turned in the direction of Jesse's flashlight beam. There was a brand-new light outside in the crevice. It was coming this way.

"Hello?" A man's voice.

Someone stepped through the entrance. He kept his flashlight pointed low, so it was easy to see his face in the beam of Jesse's light.

Hank.

I knew the next question. What are *you* doing here? But before the aunts had a chance to ask it, Hank volunteered an answer.

"I've been sitting out there on the slope for the last half hour," he said, "watching all the action. What's going on? Did you move the reunion down here?"

Ivy's voice trembled as she answered. "That's not funny, Hank."

Hank's voice came back as serious as hers. "No, I guess not."

His flashlight swept slowly over the faces in our little group. Ivy. Edna. Natalie. Jesse. Me. We looked pasty and shaky in the artificial light. Then he aimed the beam around the rest of the cavern, carefully searching the walls and floor. Finally, he focused on the passage into the next cavern. He took a deep breath and headed toward it.

"Where are you going?" I asked.

"Rat hunting," he muttered. "Wait here."

He disappeared into the passage.

"Rats?" squealed Natalie. "There are *rats* in here?"

"Not real rats," I told her. I started to add, "Just one big human rat," but stopped. Too hard to explain.

A new moan came from Aunt Edna.

"Are you all right?" asked Aunt Ivy, sounding concerned now.

"I fell and scraped my elbow, coming down into the crevice," said Aunt Edna. "I need to sit down."

Jesse and I helped her over to the only place where the cave wall was flat and smooth enough to lean against. It was right below where the fluttering usually happened. We helped Aunt Edna settle herself on the floor, resting her back against the wall.

"I believe I'll join you, Edna," said Aunt Ivy, dropping down beside her sister. "I'm feeling a little peaky myself."

We waited together – an odd, silent little group huddled together in the darkness. Suddenly, we heard a scuffling sound, along with angry male voices, inside the second cavern.

"What's that?" Aunty Ivy sounded alarmed.

"I think it's the rat Hank was looking for." I aimed my flashlight at the passage. A bald head popped through, followed by a sweatsuit-clad body.

"Archie, dear!" cried Aunt Ivy. A second later, Hank followed, his right hand a tight fist gripping the neck of Archie's sweatshirt. "Hank! What's gotten into you? What are you doing to poor Archie?"

Aunt Ivy had her flashlight trained on Hank's face. It looked tired and sort of caved in with sadness. Hank just shook his head. I waited for him to tell the aunties the truth, but he didn't. Couldn't, maybe.

Somebody had to.

"Aunt Ivy?" I said finally. "Aunt Edna? This *isn't* Uncle Archie."

CHAPTER

T HE SILENCE THAT FOLLOWED MUST HAVE LASTED a full minute.

"Not –" said Aunty Ivy. Her flashlight beam moved slowly over to Archie's face. Or, rather, it moved to where Archie's face *would* have been if he hadn't been hanging his head.

"Archie?" said Aunt Ivy. "Dear?"

Archie's shoulders wriggled a little, but he didn't answer.

"Oh my," said Aunt Ivy softly.

Aunt Edna broke in. "I don't understand a thing that's going on! If this isn't Archie, then who in heaven's name is it?"

I shone my flashlight on the one person who might be able to answer. "Hank? Do you know?"

"No," he said. "But I plan to find out. Let's get this fellow back to the house. He's got some explaining to do."

It was a long hike back. The aunties weren't fast walkers, and Hank had to keep a grip on the fake Archie, so he wasn't moving fast either. Jesse and Natalie and I led the way, with Natalie asking a whole lot of questions we couldn't answer.

"How did you know Uncle Archie was a fake? Who is he, Stevie? Why is he here? How could he fool the aunts? Where's the real Uncle Archie?"

I thought of reminding her about the three dollars I was paying her to keep quiet. But then I remembered how she'd acted in the cave. It had taken a lot of nerve to charge a mysterious creature moaning in the dark. Sure, it turned out to be just Aunty Edna, but Natalie didn't know that.

I guess it's like my mom says. Everyone has at least one or two good qualities.

The house was blazing with lights when we got back. There was a whole lot of squealing and hugging as we walked in. I won't bore you with the details except to say that Jesse and I only *thought* we'd gotten away quietly. Between us — then Ivy, then Edna — we'd managed to wake up half the household, who then woke up everybody else. The result was a whole bunch of bleary-eyed relatives sitting around the living room in their housecoats, blinking and trying to figure out what was going on. Even the twins were there. They were wearing matching pajamas — blue with little sailboats.

Hank took charge. He sat Archie down in the easy chair. "Okay, you!" said Hank. "These good people deserve an explanation."

There was a long silence, during which Uncle Archie's head, which was already drooping low, drooped farther. He seemed to be memorizing the shape of his shoes.

"Stevie?" asked my mom. "What's going on?"

"Uncle Archie isn't … Uncle Archie," I told her.

Hank nodded, backing me up. "I knew it the moment I laid eyes on him."

All heads turned to stare at the fake Uncle Archie, who hadn't so much as twitched a muscle. Aunt Ivy crept over and laid a soft hand on his arm. Tilting her head to one side, she said gently, "If you're not our Archie, we'd surely like to know who you are."

The bald head slowly lifted, and the imposter looked into Ivy's eyes. Whatever he saw there convinced him to speak.

"It's true," he said, looking around. "I'm not Archie Cooper. And I'm sorry I deceived you. You seem like a … a nice family."

"Hhrrrrmmph!" Aunt Edna's eyes flashed like a dragon's. "Who the blazes are you then? And where's our Archie?"

"Archie's in Europe," said the man, "traveling with the Radzlinsky Circus. That's where we met. We worked there together – as clowns. My name is Buddy Nestlebaum. Archie and I were a real pair. Archie and Buddy, Buddy and Archie – that was us. We chummed around together and worked together and shared a trailer and … well, people said we even looked alike. That's how I got this idea."

"What idea?" asked Ivy.

"To take Archie's place. See, Archie talked about his family all the time – about you, Ivy, and you, Edna, and all the rest of you. He was always talking about how much he missed you and how

161

much he wanted to come back here to Catriola Island. But he couldn't."

"Why not?" asked Jesse.

Buddy held out both hands in a shrug. "I don't know. Some kind of trouble. He wouldn't talk about it."

My mother, still blinking from being woken up, frowned. "I don't understand. Why would you want to *pretend* to be Uncle Archie? Why are you here?"

Buddy didn't answer. Finally, Hank answered for him. "He heard about the gold."

"Gold?" Aunt Cheryl glanced around in confusion. "You mean that old nonsense about the Klondike gold? But that's just a story ... isn't it?"

Buddy shook his head. "Archie didn't think so. He said he'd found the cave where it was hidden. He told me he had drawn a map of its location inside one of his favorite childhood books."

"*The Adventures of Tom Sawyer*," said Jesse.

Buddy grunted. "I heard about that gold for years! Finally, I made up my mind. If Archie wasn't going to come and get it ... well, I was. I looked like him, didn't I? I knew all about his family, didn't I? I deserved a break, didn't I? Why couldn't *I* be Archie Cooper for long enough to pick up that sack of gold nuggets? But I couldn't find the book." He stared accusingly at me and Jesse. "You kids had it, didn't you?"

I nodded.

"I turned those bookshelves upside down and inside out. I looked everywhere for that book. Couldn't find it. So I went out and searched the island instead. I tried to find the cave just by looking around – from some hints Archie had dropped."

"Those 'fresh air' disappearances of yours," I said.

He nodded. "It's a well-hidden cave. I couldn't find it. Not until tonight, when I finally found the book." He stared hard at me, then at Jesse.

"And?" said Hank.

"And what?" said Buddy. "That's all I know. Except that after going to so much trouble to locate the cave, I find out tonight that half the Cooper family knew exactly where it was all along! Not just Stevie and Jesse – but you, Ivy, and you, Edna. You too, Hank. I don't know if there's any gold in that cave, but it sure isn't a *secret*."

My mom rubbed her face. Her hair was sticking up funny on one side of her head where she'd slept on it. She looked straight at Buddy.

"Thank you for telling us the truth," she said quietly. "Whatever your motives, it's good to know the whole story. Aunt Ivy? Aunt Edna? I don't think there's anything more we can do about this now, do you? Let's get these kids back to bed. We can talk about it in the morning."

Some of the relatives started to get to their feet, but I put up a hand. "Mom?"

"Yes, Stevie?"

"We *don't* know the whole story. Not even close."

"What do you mean?"

I glanced over at Jesse. He nodded back.

I turned to face the group – all those relatives, yawning and gaping and blinking like owls.

163

"We've solved one mystery here," I said. "But there's a much bigger mystery still to be solved. Aunt Ivy knows what I mean. Aunt Edna too. And Hank."

"What are you talking about?" My mom sounded impatient. But she sat down again.

It was Jesse who answered. "That fateful night," he said in a dark, gloomy voice. "That fateful night forty-five years ago when ... *something happened.*"

I nodded. There was no stopping now. "The night before the real Uncle Archie ran away to join the circus. The night Orville Frisk disappeared ... and was never seen again."

"Orville Frisk?" said my mom. "Who's Or –"

She stopped when she saw Ivy's face. And Edna's. And Hank's. All three of them looked as if they'd been slapped.

"What's going on here?" asked Aunt Patricia, alarmed.

Aunt Ivy looked slowly around the room. She nodded a couple of times to herself and then said, "Stevie's right. It's time the truth came out. No, Edna, let me speak. They deserve to hear it."

CHAPTER

AUNTY IVY FOLDED HER HANDS IN HER LAP AND began to tell us her story. That's how I think of it now, looking back – as Ivy's story. May as well call it that here:

IVY'S STORY

"I adored Archie when I was a girl," she said. "He was always my big, strong, brave brother, and he never minded me following him around. I even tagged along with him and Hank when they went on nature hikes with Orville Frisk. Orville was this very pleasant – or so we thought – young man who was visiting the island to study our plant life. He stayed with us for about a month. Hank and Archie took him everywhere he wanted to go."

She reached out and patted Hank's hand. He didn't move. It was as if he'd been turned to stone.

"And then we found out that Orville wasn't being entirely … honest with us. He was here to look for the gold. He was using the boys – Hank and Archie – to help him find it.

"Archie was upset when he found this out. Worse than upset, in fact. He was very angry. Orville moved out of our house immediately, but he didn't leave the island. And that's how things stood on that ... that fateful night, as you put it, Jesse. Forty-five years ago. The night of the community dance."

She held up a thin hand, gesturing toward the window. "It was a night very much like tonight. Clear. Moonlit. A bright, beautiful summer night. I was sixteen, it was my first dance, and – oh, I was so looking forward to it. Archie drove Edna and me there in our father's old Pontiac. For the first hour, we danced and drank punch, and it was as wonderful as I ever imagined it might be."

Aunt Ivy's hands dropped into her lap and lay there like a couple of dead birds. "After that, every-thing changed ... forever. Orville Frisk showed up at the dance. It wasn't five minutes before he and Archie were having a terrible argument – right in front of everyone. Archie started ordering Orville off the island, and Orville told Archie it was a free country, and ... well, it was dreadful. They started pushing each other around. They even knocked over some punch glasses. Finally they were told to ... to take their fight outside.

"So that's what they did. When I went out a few minutes later, they were gone. Both of them! I went back inside, but ... well, the dance was totally spoiled for me. I couldn't enjoy it. I was too frightened. Hank came along a little later, and when I told him what had happened, he ran off too. I couldn't find Edna either. I waited and waited for Archie to come back to drive me home, but he never did. So there I was, left all alone at my very first dance. A neighbor was kind enough to drive me home."

Aunt Ivy wrung her hands together in her lap. A tear forced its way out of her right eye and trickled slowly down her cheek.

"Later that night, I heard the back door open. I went downstairs and met Archie as he came in. He was … he was terribly upset. He told me he had to leave Catriola. Forever. I asked him why, of course, and he … he told me.

"He said that when he and Orville left the dance, they headed for Bat Cave. That's what they were fighting about. It seems that they had each found the cave a few days earlier – separately. They were both convinced the gold was hidden inside. All they had to do was search carefully, and they'd find it.

"So they ended up facing each other that night – still angry – on the slope just above the crevice. They started pushing each other around, even throwing punches. But it was the wrong place to fight. Especially at night. The wrong place!"

Aunt Ivy looked around desperately, as if hoping we could somehow change what had happened.

"On one of Orville's punches … Archie ducked and … Orville pitched forward, right into the crevice."

"He fell in?" asked Jesse.

Aunt Ivy nodded. "It's a long drop. There are so many sharp rocks at the bottom. It wasn't Archie's fault! Archie called down to Orville, but there was no answer. So Archie climbed down into the crevice and …"

She paused for so long that I thought she had stopped.

"The poor man was dead," she said finally. "He must have hit his head. Archie put his ear to Orville's mouth to listen for breathing, but … well, there wasn't any."

We all sat there without moving, just taking it in. After forty-five years of avoiding and hiding and pretending, Orville Frisk's fate was finally out in the open.

"Poor Archie was in a great panic." Aunt Ivy sighed, wiping at her cheek. "He ran all the way home. He wasn't much more than a boy, really. It was an accident! But everyone at the dance had heard him arguing with Orville. Archie was terrified he'd be sent to jail and the family would be disgraced. It was the wrong thing to do, of course – running away. I tried to stop him. I said people would believe him if only he told the truth … but I couldn't convince him. He left on the ferry a few hours later."

Aunt Ivy reached into her pocket, pulled out a tissue and blew her nose.

"After he was gone, I couldn't help thinking about poor Orville Frisk. His body lying in that crevice. It wasn't right. Archie had told me about the map in *Tom Sawyer*, so I found the book, and … and I *forced* myself to go to Bat Cave. I don't know what I was thinking. I suppose I had some idea I might bury him."

She looked around, startled, as if surprised we were still there.

"He was gone," she said simply, holding out her hands, palms up. "Orville Frisk's body had disappeared. I … well, I didn't know what to think. I still don't! I've had nightmares about it ever since … about Archie, about the gold, about poor Orville Frisk. Forty-five long years … and I *still* have no idea what happened to the body."

She folded her hands, finished. A hush hung over the room – the echo of forty-five years of silence. It was broken finally by a sound like a rusty hinge. Hank was clearing his throat.

"I … well, I believe I can add to Ivy's story," he said. "You see … I was there too, out on the ridge, on that fateful night. Only, Archie didn't know it."

CHAPTER

16

HANK TOOK ONE GNARLED HAND IN THE OTHER and cracked a knuckle. Then he cracked three or four more. Finally, he leaned both arms on the back of the chair he was straddling and began to tell us a story. I think of it now – looking back – as Hank's story. I may as well call it that:

HANK'S STORY

"On the night of the dance, I arrived late at the community hall. When I got there, Ivy told me what had happened. She said Archie had been arguing with Orville Frisk and the two of them had run off. I knew right away they must have gone to Bat Cave. Archie and I had found it a couple of days earlier. Orville had followed us there – that's how he 'found' it. Archie warned him to stay away, but he wouldn't.

"When I heard they'd left the dance, I figured I'd better go after them. Those two together – at the cave? At night? Nothing but trouble.

"But when I got to the cave, there was no sign of anyone. Not until I was standing right above the crevice. That's when I heard the moaning."

"M-moaning?" stammered Jesse.

Hank nodded. "It was coming from the crevice. I crawled down inside, and that's where I found him. Orville Frisk."

"Dead?" asked Jesse.

"No!" said Hank. "I told you – he was moaning. He was trying to crawl out of the crevice, but he couldn't. His arm was hurt. Busted maybe. He said I owed it to him to help him, because it was *my* partner who had pushed him into the crevice. Archie had shoved him in there, he said, and left him for dead."

"That's a lie!" cried Ivy.

Hank nodded. "It sure didn't sound like the Archie I knew. But I couldn't just leave Orville there, hurt as he was. I helped him out. I even offered to take him home.

"Trouble was – old Orville was still madder than a nest of hornets. As soon as we got to the top of the crevice, he started arguing with *me*. Picking a fight! His one arm was probably broken from his fall, but he was using the other one to poke me in the chest.

"I told him to cut it out. But he kept poking and poking and poking, and the two of us were up there dancing around, with me trying to stay out of his way – just above that crevice. And you won't believe it, but ..."

Natalie said it for him. "He fell into the crevice again?"

Hank nodded.

"Oy!" said Jesse, smacking his forehead. "He fell into the same hole *twice* in the same night? The guy must have been taking stupid pills."

"Oh, he wasn't stupid." Hank shook his head. "Just mean, that's all. Rattlesnake mean. Even so, I couldn't leave him down there. So I crawled in after him again."

Hank hunched his shoulders up around his ears. His face had lost some color, and I noticed a thin sheen of sweat across his forehead. "This time," he said, "there was no moaning."

His voice cracked. "No breathing either."

Looking straight at Ivy, he said, "It was me who should have run away the next day. Not Archie! Orville's death was *my* fault."

"Now then, Hank." Aunt Ivy reached out her thin hand to hold his big one. "Don't say that. It wasn't your fault. He fell! It was an accident."

"Nobody could ever blame you, Hank," added my mom.

"Well, *I* blame me." Hank looked about as miserable as a person can look. "I've been driving myself crazy over this – for forty-five years. I keep thinking that if I hadn't been so eager to find that gold ..."

It was as if he carried the weight of those forty-five years right there on his bony shoulders. No wonder he always looked so unhappy – especially the last few days.

"When I saw that he was dead, I ran home," said Hank. "I shouldn't have, I know. But I was so frightened. The next morning, in daylight, I went back ... but it was just like Ivy said. The body was gone. Disappeared into thin air! I went looking for Archie, hoping *he* could make sense of it. Archie and I – we were friends, you see, but Archie was the thinker. I figured he'd know what to do. But –"

"Archie was gone," interrupted Natalie. "Right?"

Hank nodded. "Ivy told me he'd run off to – to join the circus, of all things. What had gotten into him? Arch had never in his whole life said one word about joining a circus. He'd never even *seen* a circus!

"Without Archie to do the thinking, I guess I was a bit lost. I ended up doing ... nothing. It was the biggest mistake of my life. I've regretted it ever since."

"You were just a boy," said Ivy softly, still holding his hand. "Like Archie."

Hank shook his head. "I knew better. Even if it was an accident, I should have reported it to the police." He looked straight at Ivy, and I could see that his eyes were full of tears. "I know those nightmares of yours, Ivy. I get them too. All the time."

Jesse frowned. He opened his mouth, closed it, then opened it again. "Wait a minute. I still don't get it. What happened to the body?"

Hank continued to stare at Ivy. His shoulders rose slowly in a baffled shrug.

Ivy shrugged back and let out a sigh. "I suppose that will remain a mystery."

Suddenly Aunt Edna broke in. "No, it won't!"

Everyone turned to face her. Her voice was hoarse and scratchy, as if she didn't use it much.

"I know the whole truth," she said slowly. "I can tell you *exactly* what happened to Orville Frisk on that fateful night."

CHAPTER

AUNT EDNA SQUINTED AT US, THEN RUBBED HER EYES. "Has anyone seen my glasses?" Most of us had never seen Aunty Edna *wearing* her glasses, so we didn't even know what to look for. Aunty Ivy, once she got over her shock, ran into the kitchen and came back with a pair of metal-rimmed oval glasses.

Aunty Edna put them on. She looked around as if she was seeing us for the first time. Personally, I couldn't understand why she didn't like to wear the glasses; she looked much better with them on. She didn't have to squint, so you could see more of her eyes. They were a nice blue-green color.

The relatives leaned forward in their chairs, eager to hear the third – and last, I hoped – story about that fateful night. Aunt Edna, her face flushed, her voice halting, began:

EDNA'S STORY

"I was at the dance that night too," she said. "I went there all dreamy-eyed, my heart full of

crazy hopes. None of my family knew it but ...
I was ... in love with Orville Frisk."

There was a loud gasp to my left. My mom
covered her mouth with her hands. Nobody else
had actually gasped, but most of the relatives'
mouths were hanging open. Aunt Ivy looked
more shocked than anyone.

Aunt Edna's hands trembled slightly as she continued. "I went to the dance that night expecting
to waltz the evening away with the man I loved.
Instead, I watched as he got into a terrible
argument – with my own brother.

"It was awful – just awful. After they left, I waited
around for a long time. I kept hoping Orville
would come back, and we'd dance and dance,
the way I'd dreamed. The waltz, the foxtrot, the
tango ..."

Aunt Edna paused for a moment and swayed
slightly, caught up in her memories. "When Orville
didn't come back, I went looking for him. I ran
down to where he was living – in a tent on the
beach. He wasn't there, so I headed for Bat Cave."

Hank cut in, confused. "But Edna, how did *you*
know about Bat Cave? I thought only me and
Archie and Orville knew."

"I knew *exactly* where the cave was," said
Edna. "I'd already been there ... twice. With
Orville. I was ... helping him search for the gold."

Aunt Ivy sat up straight, a look of horror on her
face. "Edna! You didn't! Against your own brother?"

Edna stared at her sister, unblinking, through
the glasses. "I did, Ivy, and I'm not proud of it.

But I'm trying to tell you the truth now. Please! Let me finish."

She gazed around with a pleading look on her face. "I'd never been in love before. Orville was the most exciting man I'd ever met. Helping him look for the gold seemed like an adventure! And I could be near him, and ..."

Hank nodded. "Go on, Edna. Tell us what happened when you went to the cave that night."

Edna swallowed, then continued. "Archie must have already run off when I arrived. But you were still there, Hank. I was up on the ridge when you had *your* fight with Orville. I saw the whole thing! I saw him poking you. I saw him fall into the crevice, and I watched you climb down to help him ... and then come out alone. I was running along the ridge, calling out! But the wind was against me, and you couldn't hear. I had only moonlight to guide my way, and again and again, I tripped over roots and branches and fell. By the time I got down to the crevice, you were gone."

Hank gulped, white-faced. "So you found ... the body?"

"No!" The word exploded out of Aunt Edna's mouth. "There *was* no body! Orville Frisk was lying at the bottom of that crevice all right. But he was smoking a cigarette and laughing!"

"Smo –" Hank was so shocked he couldn't even finish the word.

"Laughing!" Edna repeated. "He told me he had played a great trick on you and Archie – a trick that would keep you both out of his hair."

"Frisk was still alive?" squeaked Jesse. "I don't get it! Archie and Hank both listened for his breathing."

I thought fast. "He was holding his breath, wasn't he, Aunt Edna? He wanted them to believe he was dead – and that it was their fault."

Edna nodded. "Orville *played* dead … just like the dog he was. You should have checked his pulse, Hank – although, who knows? The man was so wily, maybe he could have faked that too."

Jesse stared. "So it was all a big trick? To keep Archie and Hank away from the cave?"

Edna nodded again. "Orville's exact words were, 'Those boys will be running scared for weeks, Edna … as long as *you* help me.'"

Nobody could think of a thing to say. We all realized what must have happened. Edna had done what he asked. Helped him. Against her own brother. Against Hank.

"Orville stayed clear of the cave the next day," she continued, "thinking Archie or Hank might come back, looking for his body. But after that – well, for the next week, he camped inside the cave, searching for the gold. Fool that I was, I brought him supplies. Food. Water. Candles. Blankets. Even cigarettes."

Jesse turned to me. "We found old cigarette butts in the cave, didn't we, Stevie? And some old chicken bones."

Natalie leaned forward eagerly. "Did he find it, Aunt Edna? The gold?"

Aunt Edna sniffed. "What gold? I don't believe

there ever *was* any gold on this island. Orville searched Bat Cave from one end to the other. He never found a thing.

"Finally, he gave up. He asked me to help him sneak off the island. He wanted me to borrow a motorboat and take him across to the mainland. So that's what I did, one evening after dark. Orville said he would send for me as soon as he got set up in business. He even carved our initials – his and mine – in a heart inside the cave."

"We saw that," I told her. "Or, at least, we saw the heart. There weren't any initials in it."

"I scratched them out," said Aunt Edna. "Orville Frisk never did come back. He never so much as wrote me a letter. He was a con man through and through – lying, thieving, scheming and conniving. When I finally figured *that* out, I got so mad I went back to the cave and scratched out those initials."

Edna sighed. Her whole body sagged. Suddenly I remembered the book she'd been hiding – a romance!

"Orville Frisk tricked Archie," she said finally. "He tricked Hank too. And most of all, he tricked … me."

She took off her glasses and rubbed her eyes. Was she crying? Aunt Edna? When she put the glasses back on, her eyes were pink around the edges. "I've been sorry ever since. Oh, not about Orville. *He* was no great loss. But I've been so sorry about deceiving my family. If I'd had a chance to talk to Archie before he ran off, I might have told him the truth. But he left the next morning before I was awake. I might have told you the truth too, Hank. But you didn't come near our house for months."

"Too upset," mumbled Hank. "I didn't want to talk to anyone."

Aunt Edna nodded. She glanced at Aunt Ivy, almost timidly.

"Ivy?" she said in a tiny voice, nothing like her regular one. "Can you forgive me?"

Aunt Ivy suddenly turned into a faucet. Collapsing into Edna's arms, she started sobbing so hard you couldn't tell what she was saying, but the general meaning came across – yes, she forgave Aunty Edna. Aunt Edna started sobbing then too, and that made Hank put his arms around both of them. He didn't actually cry, but he had that wet-eyed, ready-to-blubber look.

"Tell me when it's over," muttered Jesse in my ear. "I can't *stand* this stuff!"

Fortunately, it didn't last long. Someone thought it was a good idea to make tea, and various relatives hugged Aunty Edna and Aunty Ivy and Hank. Kevin (or maybe Kenneth) thought it would be a good idea to hug *me* – until I set him straight. We all drank tea, and I don't know whether it was the tea or the confessing or the crying, but both aunts looked a whole lot better than … well, than I'd ever seen them.

"It's as if a weight has been lifted from my shoulders," said Aunt Edna, looking around with a nervous smile.

"I hope I'll finally stop having those nightmares," said Aunt Ivy in a voice that was still sort of trembly.

She turned to Buddy Nestlebaum, who had sat there through all these stories not saying a word. Someone had handed him a cup of tea, and he sipped at it thoughtfully.

"Mr. Nestlebaum? Buddy?" said Aunt Ivy. "We would like our Archie – the real Archie – to come home to us. As you can see, there's no earthly reason for him to stay away any longer. Can you help us?"

Buddy put down his cup and saucer with a clatter and rose to his feet. "Ivy, I was thinking the exact same thing. I would be happy – and honored – to help you find Archie and bring him home."

"It's the *least* you can do," said Natalie sourly, adding under her breath, "you old fake."

Jesse caught my eye, and we grinned at each other. Natalie had spoken for us too.

My mom started clearing cups and spoons. "I'm exhausted," she said, to no one in particular. "Now that everything's settled, can we *please* go back to bed?"

Outside the window, the sky was beginning to lighten with the dawn. I glanced over at my mom. She *did* look tired, and I hated to keep her from sleeping. But there was one thing left to say. And maybe do.

"Excuse me?" I said. My mom was the only one who heard, so I repeated it, louder. "Excuse me – everybody! We still haven't found the Klondike gold!"

Heads turned. The cup-clinking stopped. My mom gave me one of those I-can't-believe-I'm-hearing-this looks.

"But, Stephanie," said Aunt Edna, "there's no such thing."

"Sorry, Aunt Edna. I don't agree. I think there *is* lost gold. And I think I know where to find it."

CHAPTER

I WAS ON MY OWN. NOT EVEN JESSE KNEW WHAT I was talking about. My mom heaved a great sigh and dropped back down into her chair.

"Okay, Stevie. Make it quick."

The relatives drifted back to their places in the living room. I waited, feeling a little tense, until everyone was listening. It was one of those times in a detective's life when you have to take a risk – go out on a limb. Maybe you're right … maybe you're wrong … you don't know. But you have to give it a shot. And it's important to at least *sound* like you know what you're talking about.

"Aunt Edna?" I said. "Aunt Ivy? Could you stand up?"

Puzzled, the aunts rose to their feet.

"Could you turn around, please?"

They turned. I pointed at their backs. Faint smudges of clay stained both their shirts.

"There it is," I said. "The clue to the location of the gold."

Nobody spoke. The relatives stared at me blankly.

"Look, it's really hard to explain, and –" I decided to be honest. "– and I may be totally wrong. But I think I can show you where the gold is hidden. Back at the cave."

"At the cave?" said my mom. "Now? It's the middle of the night."

I pointed out the window at the breaking dawn. "Not anymore."

She let out a sigh. "Honestly, Stevie! Can't it wait?"

I didn't answer. I just turned and stared at Buddy Nestlebaum. Everyone else stared at him too.

"What?" said Buddy, looking around in a panic. "You don't think *I* would –"

From the looks on the relatives' faces, it was clear they *did* believe he would do something crooked. Sneak off, maybe, to search for the gold, while the rest of us slept.

Hank rose to his feet. "May as well get started. It's a long walk."

So that's how it happened that as the sun rose over Catriola Island, a long line of Cooper relatives, plus Jesse, Hank and Buddy, walked through the forest toward Bat Cave.

"Ouch!" said Natalie as she stubbed her toe on a root. "You'd better be right, Stevie Diamond. That's all I have to say."

If that was *really* all she had to say, I would have been thrilled. But, of course, there was more. Much more. I escaped to the head of the line and joined Hank. A bundle of tools, tied together with a rope, was resting on his shoulder – shovel, pick, crowbar. Aunty Ivy had shown him where to find the tools after I told her we'd need them.

"Care to explain what we're going to do with these?" asked Hank.

I shook my head. "But I have a question for you. How come you showed up at the cave last night, Hank? How did you know we'd be there?"

"Saw the flashlights from my house," he said. "I've been watching the ridge area ever since Buddy showed up. I knew he wasn't Archie, and I had a pretty good idea what he was after. I figured he'd turn up at the cave sooner or later."

"You've been watching the ridge all along?" I said. "Daytime too?"

"Daytime too. As much as I could manage anyway."

"Did you see Jesse and me ..."

Hank chuckled. "Does this sound familiar?" He cupped his hands over his mouth and moaned in a low, ghostly voice, "Goooooooo hooooooome."

"Iiiy! Was that you?" I gave him a little push. "Do you know how scary that was?"

"I *wanted* to scare you," he said. "I didn't want you kids and Buddy meeting up at the cave some time when I wasn't around."

"Well, thanks ... I guess," I said.

Finally, we reached the ridge. The rising sun lit up the distant city with a pale yellow glow. The water in the strait was dead calm, and the slope tumbled down beneath bits of morning mist that hovered like fairy wisps.

But this was no time to admire the scenery. Hank led us along the ridge and down the slope toward the arbutus tree and the cave.

When my mom saw the crevice, she flipped out. "*This* is where you've been coming, Stevie? And you, Jesse? Look at those rocks on the bottom. Why, someone could get *killed* –"

Suddenly, she realized what she was saying. She noticed, too, that everyone was staring at her. "I mean –" she said lamely, and then, "Oh, forget it." She started letting herself down into the crevice backward.

It took a while, but finally we were all at the bottom of the crevice, jostling against one another in the narrow space. I took out my flashlight and led the way into the cave.

I don't know whether there really is safety in numbers, but it sure *felt* safer to have my whole family along. I didn't get a single goose bump – not even when we got close to the passage and the strange fluttering started up. I figured that if there *were* bats, they'd have so many heads of curly Cooper hair to choose from, there was only a small chance they'd go after mine.

Stopping just outside the passage, I pointed my flashlight at the lower part of the wall – the only smooth flat surface in the cave. The place Aunt Edna and Aunt Ivy had leaned against last night.

"Well, Stevie?" said my mom.

Taking a deep breath, I rubbed my palm along the smooth part of the wall. Then I shone the light on my palm to show it to the others.

"Look! Clay. The same stuff that's on the backs of Aunt Ivy's and Aunt Edna's shirts."

"So?" Jesse's voice, out of the gloom.

"So it's the only clay surface in the whole cave. Touch some of the other surfaces – you'll see." I shone my flashlight around. A few of the relatives reached out and touched the stone walls.

"So why is that?" I said. "Why is there only one small flat area of clay in a whole cave of lumpy stone? I think it's because the clay was *put* there – on purpose. I think someone hauled clay into this cave to block up a tunnel."

Hank pushed his way through the group. He shone his flashlight carefully around the edges of the smooth flat area. Leaning over until his nose practically touched the surface, he started scraping away with a fingernail.

"Stevie's right," he said in an excited voice. "The clay's the same color as the stone in the rest of the cave, so you can't *see* where it starts and ends. But if you touch it, you can *feel* the difference."

My mom's voice interrupted, confused. "But who'd want to seal off a tunnel with clay?"

"Someone who wanted to hide something," I said, "and seal it off so no one else would find it."

"The Klondike gold thief!" I heard Jesse's fingers snap in the darkness. "The guy who snuck off the ship and hid the gold in this cave, hoping to come back for it later."

"Exactly!" I said. "And since the tunnel is still blocked off, he probably never did come back."

"What are we waiting for?" asked Hank, reaching for the pick. "Stand back, everyone."

Aunt Edna and Aunt Ivy and my mom backed right off, all the way out to the crevice. The rest of us hovered, just inside the entrance.

Ka-whack! went the pick, followed by the sound of falling rubble.

"It's working!" yelled a twin.

Hank grunted. "Just clay," he said. "Easy to break up."

Aunt Cheryl and Aunt Patricia pitched in. Aunt Cheryl worked the clay loose with the crowbar, while Aunt Patricia pulled the rubble away with the shovel. The rest of us waited, listening to the thunking and scraping sounds.

"Jesse?" Kevin (or maybe Kenneth) was hanging on to Jesse's arm. He sounded nervous. "Are there really ... bats in this cave?"

"Don't worry about it," said Jesse. "Even if there are, they won't hurt you."

I cleared my throat loudly. Jesse pretended not to notice.

"People have a lot of funny ideas about bats," he went on, sounding a lot like Mr. Van den Verk, our science teacher. "They think, for instance, that bats will get tangled in their hair."

"Don't they?"

"Nah." Jesse let out a little chuckle. "The only reason a bat would come near you is to eat a bug that's hanging around your head. Bats eat mosquitoes. They *help* us."

I groaned. Jesse ignored me.

"I thought bats were vampires," said the other twin. "I thought they *bit* people."

"There are no vampire bats around here," said Jesse cheerfully. "They live in South America and Central America. They don't usually pick on people anyway. They go after animals and –"

I couldn't stand it anymore. "Stop right there, Jesse Kulniki! Since when did you become a bat expert?"

I could hear the smile in his voice. "Since I looked them up in the encyclopedia last night, Stevie. While we were waiting for Buddy to make his move. I didn't want to say anything, not after I made such a fuss. But it's true. Bats are our friends."

Friends? I was glad Jesse was over his bat phobia. But "friends" was going a little *too* far.

There was a loud *whunk* from across the cavern as the pick hit the wall.

"Hey! Look at this!" yelled Hank.

We all rushed over to where Hank was pointing, at a small opening in the clay about the size of a volleyball. Watery light shone through from the other side.

Hank gouged at the opening with the shovel, enlarging it so that it was big enough to crawl through. Then he stood back and waited.

"Stevie?" he said, holding out an arm toward the hole. "This was your discovery. Would you like to do the honors?"

Me? I didn't know whether to be thrilled or scared. I compromised by being both. Stepping forward, I got down on my hands and knees and crawled toward the hole Hank had made. When I got there, I stuck my head through.

It was another cavern. But a small one this time. About the size of a bathroom. Above me, in the ceiling, there was a long thin crack – too thin for a person to get through – filled with sunlight. The moment my head was inside, I understood the fluttering.

Birds! Dozens of them, perched all over the walls in nests stuck in cracks and holes. When they saw my head, they rose in waves, fluttering their wings, chirping a *tri-tri* sound, and flying one by one out the crack into the daylight.

I forced my way inside. Phew! The place was a giant bird's nest, and birds' nests don't smell that great – or look that great either.

Jesse was right behind me.

"Swallows!" he said as he crawled in beside me. He pointed to a couple of birds who had decided to wait out our invasion and were still perched on ledges.

Hank's head poked through the hole. "How're you kids doing?

"Fine," I said. "But it's pretty small in here. Ugh! Stinky too. I don't think there's room for the rest of you."

"You got *that* right," said Hank, peering around. "We'll wait back here."

"Start looking," I told Jesse, who was checking out the nests. "We don't want to spend any more time in here than we have to."

The floor of this cavern was messy with bird droppings. We tiptoed around, using our flashlights to search.

"Stevie?" Jesse's voice was quivery with excitement. "Come here."

I ran over. He had his left hand crammed into a crack in the wall. He was pulling something out. Some kind of cloth, dirty and crusted and half rotted. As I watched, he slowly, carefully pulled out – a small round sack.

"It's heavy, Stevie."

I could hardly breathe. "Quick. Let's show the others."

We scooted back through the tunnel. When the relatives saw the sack, there was a chorus of oohs and ahs. Jesse squatted and set the sack down on the cave floor. It was about the size of a lunch bag. With so many flashlights on it, it looked as if it was lit up by a spotlight.

We waited.

"Stevie? Jesse?" said Hank. "Who's going to open it?"

We opened it together. I fumbled with the top, which was caked over with muck. Jesse pulled the sack open. Then I reached inside and pulled out a small lump. It was pretty gnarly looking, full of bumps and holes, but there was no mistaking it.

"Gold!" said Jesse.

CHAPTER

S OMEBODY WHISTLED.
Somebody else said, "Whoo-hoo!"
Aunt Edna's voice boomed out of the darkness. "Well, if anyone's got a feather, you can knock
me over with it!"

"The lost gold," said Aunt Ivy in a half whisper.
"So it was really here ... all these years."

Jesse reached inside the bag and brought out
more lumps – a whole bunch of them. Aunt Ivy
suddenly burst into tears, and then the hugging
started up again. Why was it that in every important
moment in this family, everybody had to *hug*
everybody else?

"Sheesh!" muttered Jesse, wriggling out of an
Aunt-Edna hug.

The walk back was way quicker than the walk
there, with everybody talking and laughing.
Along the way, somebody – Aunt Cheryl, I think
– said we should maybe check to see that the
lumps really *were* gold.

So as soon as we got back, Aunt Ivy phoned a
retired geologist who lived on the other side of

the island – Mr. Willard. He came right over, took a close look at those lumps and smiled.

"It's the real thing," he said.

After that, the word spread like wildfire. Everybody on the whole island – at least, it felt like everybody – came by to take a look. Aunt Ivy rushed around, serving homemade apple cider, and Aunt Edna made fudge. At least, that's what she said it was.

One of the people who came by was Mr. Priddy. "I knew it!" he crowed to anyone who would listen. "I knew all along it was more than a legend. How many times have I said – that gold is *here* on Catriola Island! I would have found it myself if I'd had time to look around."

I caught Jesse's eye. He grinned and shook his head.

"It was me who told these kids the story of the gold," Mr. Priddy informed Aunt Ivy as he followed her into the kitchen. "I gave them suggestions for finding Bat Cave too. Did they tell you that?"

"Mmmm," said Aunt Ivy absentmindedly. "Have a piece of fudge, Teddy dear."

Another neighbor who came by – Maggie Santino – was a lawyer. The aunts asked her who the gold would belong to. Maggie said she was pretty sure that after all this time, the aunts could keep it. It had been on their land for a hundred years, after all. Also, according to Mr. Priddy, who had a book about the Klondike Gold Rush, the gold miner who'd been robbed had died in Seattle a year after the robbery, with no family. So it looked like there'd be no one around to make a claim.

That led to a big family discussion about what the aunts should do with the money. Aunt Cheryl thought they should go on a cruise in the Caribbean. Aunt Patricia thought they should invest it in the stock market; she offered to give them free advice. Natalie thought it would be fabulous if they bought everyone in the family new wardrobes, starting with her.

Aunt Edna and Aunt Ivy just smiled. They already knew what they wanted to do with it.

"We're going to Europe," said Aunt Ivy softly, "to find Archie."

"We've never been anywhere really!" said Aunt Edna, with a little giggle.

"What a good idea," said my mom. "You'll see Paris. Rome. London."

"And Archie," said Ivy and Edna at the same time. You could tell what really mattered to them.

"But won't you have some money left over after that?" asked Natalie, still thinking, I guess, about a new wardrobe.

"Yes, we will," said Aunt Ivy. "Edna and I would like to see it do some good. That gold has caused so much heartache over the years."

"We were thinking of a new community hall," said Edna. "The old one's practically falling down."

"Excellent idea," said Aunt Patricia.

"Very generous," agreed Hank.

"The old hall looks fine to me," muttered Natalie. No one paid any attention.

After that, Jesse and I had to start packing. We'd missed the morning ferry and were taking the evening ferry home.

A strange thing happened when it came time to say good-bye to the cousins. I actually felt a little bit sorry to leave them behind. The twins, standing there in their matching yellow jogging suits, looked sort of funny and sweet, instead of funny and weird. Natalie said "Gyahhh!" instead of "Good-bye," and Jesse and I gyahhhed her right back. And Hugo was Hugo, of course. The kiss he planted on my cheek was so wet that I needed a tissue to wipe it off.

Aunty Edna and Aunty Ivy drove us to the ferry.

"Thank you, dear Stevie," Aunt Ivy whispered as she hugged me. "You've made us so happy."

Aunt Edna gave me such a squeezy hug I couldn't breathe. When she let go, she had tears in her eyes. "Good-bye, Stevie."

I was so surprised to hear her call me Stevie, I couldn't answer.

"Good-bye, Jesse," said Aunt Edna, holding out her arms for a hug. When he stuck out his hand instead, she smiled and shook it. "You're welcome to come back any time you like."

As we turned to go aboard, Aunt Ivy handed me a brown-paper-wrapped parcel. "Open it on the ferry," she said.

I stared at the wrapping, puzzled. What could it be? The aunts had already given us tiny gold nuggets – one for Jesse and one for me – as souvenirs.

"Thanks, Aunt Ivy."

We walked onto the ferry and climbed the stairs to the top deck. Then we waved down at the aunts as the boat left the little Catriola dock.

"Don't they look great!" said my mom. "What a strain it must have been to keep those awful secrets all these years. Now that the truth is out, the aunts look … almost girlish."

It was true. They were both wearing flowered dresses. Aunty Ivy's was blue, and Aunty Edna's was yellow with peach-colored splotches. Aunt Edna was wearing her glasses too, and the evening sunlight hitting the lenses made them glint golden. The sisters had wide smiles on their faces, and they were waving like a couple of little kids – with their hands flapping up and down above their heads. Aunty Ivy started blowing kisses. After a moment, Aunty Edna joined her. Aunty Edna even used both hands!

We waved till we couldn't see them anymore.

"You kids go ahead to the cafeteria if you like," said my mom. "I'm going to stay out here for a while."

Six days of Aunt Edna's cooking had turned "cafeteria" into a beautiful word. Jesse and I ran for the lineup.

"What's in the parcel?" asked Jesse as the line moved slowly forward.

I ripped it open. Inside was *The Adventures of Tom Sawyer*. I smiled and flipped it open to the last page. There it was – the map that had led us to Bat Cave.

"They're letting us keep *Tom Sawyer*," I said. "Cool!"

"Read the card," said Jesse, pointing at the little blue thank-you card tucked inside.

I read it out loud. "'Dear Stevie and Jesse. Now that you're finished with the map, you'll have time to read Tom Sawyer's story. It was among our favorites when we were your age – and it has *caves* in it. With our love and thanks, Aunty Ivy and Aunty Edna.'"

"Caves?" Jesse looked longingly at the book. "I didn't get that far."

I handed it over. "Don't take too long to finish," I said.

"I won't."

We were at the front of the line now. I picked up a tray and edged along the counter toward the food.

"Stevie, look!" Jesse's eyes were huge.

It was like finding gold all over again. Cheeseburgers, ham croissants, french fries, chicken strips, clam chowder, Jell-O with whipped cream, chocolate cake, butterscotch pudding, strawberry cheesecake!

"What are you having?" asked Jesse.

"The special."

"Which one?" He pointed at a sign that showed two combo specials.

"Both of them," I said.

He laughed. "Both?"

"Both! That's just for starters. And … Jesse?"

"Yeah?"

Was this the right time to ask? He seemed to be in a good mood, but maybe I should wait till after we'd eaten.

Oh, what the heck.

"Listen, Jesse, Aunty Ivy told me that when they come back from Europe with the real Archie, they're going to have another Cooper family reunion, and I was wondering if you'd ..."

He held up his hand, palm out. "Your family is nuts, Stevie."

I hung my head. "I know."

"They hug too much, they cry too much, they play dumb games, and they eat weird food. And ... I'd love to come to your next family reunion."

I gawked. "You would? Really?"

"Sure!" He grinned and stuck out his hand. I shook it.

"And now," he said, reaching for a piece of cheesecake with one hand and grabbing a dough-nut with the other, "it's time to do some serious eating."

And we did.